CHIP MARTIN grew up in California and has lived mainly in London since the early 1970s. He writes criticism under the name of Stoddard Martin and is the author of a sequence of linked novellas, published by Starhaven.

The cover incorporates a photograph of the Circle X trail by Tanya Thompson. The back cover includes a photograph of the author at the Shakespeare and Company literary festival, 2010, taken by Thomas Pirel.

TRUE NORTH

three stories

by Chip Martin

©Chip Martin 2013
ISBN 0-936315-37-7

STARHAVEN, 42 Frognal, London NW3 6AG
books@starhaven.org.uk
www.starhaven.org.uk

Typeset in Dante by John Mallinson

Contents

But how can we 'find ourselves' again, and how can man 'know himself'? ... This is the most effective way: – to let the youthful soul look back on life with the question, 'What hast thou up to now truly loved? What hast drawn thy soul upward, mastered it and blessed it too?'...

Thoughts out of Season, II

THE TRIP NORTH

1.

Our daisy-stripped Beetle hummed over the Golden Gate. On both sides water shimmered under a lowering sun. The garish towers of Babylon receded out of our vision, watching us diminish with their usual cool. Up to the tunnel on the far side we sped, and vanished into its rainbow maw.

We were going north.

Lauren sat beside me stitching old moccasins. It was so like her, so productive, so thrifty, unwilling to let an hour pass by idly. It made you think of some pioneer past, some era when diligent housewives occupied themselves in such tasks out of necessity, not as creative hobbies.

We talked now and then, she in dreamy half-sentences as eczema-flecked fingers tugged at the resistant suede, then circled back to prick it again. The part of her wholly absorbed in this act made her press her lips together and bend her head low to inspect what she did. Auburn curls fell over the curve of her neck. Bringing the thread up, she would bite, then re-thread her needle and go for it again.

Residential suburbs thinned into tidier country hamlets. We passed into the next county and a long, rumpled valley where light rain had turned the hills green. Still, you could see blackened spots where burnt-out grasses recalled last summer's heat.

Curt dozed in the back with his ex's black Lab, dreams laden with TV imagery. He was hanging out on some hot dusty road in some lumber-jack town, rolling his own, nipping a hip-flask, jiving hard-boiled hookers. His sporadic snarfles punctuated the Beetle's hum. Head back, eyes flapped, brow faintly furrowed, he looked more than relaxed; narcotized maybe, decadent sure-

1

ly. He was an old tar just in from the Orient ducking in and out of the north coastal ports, running hemp, opium. Or maybe he was just some wild-haired sky-pirate, the ends of his Fu Manchu fluttering up in a breeze his raucous breath made.

The Beetle crossed over a new county line. The highway narrowed into a two-lane blacktop and rose into sweet running curves. No more flat-bedded valleys with treeless farms and vine-covered slopes; gnarled oaks bent their sinews to the earth here; manzanilla grew to a man's height above granite outcroppings. Vistas no longer clogged by products of civilization, yet not yet screened by in-trooping redwoods; weather-worn tors spoke of times futuristic, unearthly, as well as ancient days. We were halfway to the north now: north, and the more primitive woods and unsophisticated towns that clung to the coast there, towns that had prospered long before a megapolitan south had been invented; north to a world that had once thrived on fishing or lumber but now, being marked out as depressed, saw its demoralized youth flee as soon as they could to the plasticized promise we were escaping; north to a cradle of so-called counter-culture, back to a land where migration had brought scores of artisans of a 'new age', hibernees from an all-too-modern present melding into a semi-mythical past, exposing themselves only in stubborn pride on occasions like the 'gathering of the tribes' we were heading up there for. We, especially Lauren, were going north for the Eureka Crafts Fair. We, especially I, were going north to see our old buddy Hart. We, especially Curt, were going north to party; and separate anticipations burned slowly in each one of us.

It had been a year now since Hart had tossed his farewell at the City and packed it in for the north; a year since we'd rollicked a last time together and his quasi-revolutionary pronouncement 'Liberate yourselves, motherfuckers!' had echoed 'til it faded over all that we did. Hart had moved north. He was not humble and he possessed no craft. Lifestyle was the sole art he had packed with him when Otis and Randy and the others who'd made the trek already persuaded him that *north* was where it was happening, man. And Hart's transition had marked end of an era. A spark that had fired us gradually burned down. For a time, temptation to follow was strong – Curt almost did, and that chick Vanity who'd been doing a thing with Hart in the City picked up one afternoon and high-tailed it up. But then time had passed and, with new trips and people inevitably sidling in on us, the vistas began to occlude.

When people like Hart first come into your life, all the parental and academic that's gone before seems to loosen and fall. Suddenly you feel free and brash and the sole thing that matters is the potency of being young and fearlessness that comes from bursting out of the crusty old givens. But then as that phase drifted into mirage, Lauren had entered my life. Lauren of the luscious hair and plain understanding; of the intelligent eyes and a diligence that managed to tie up the loose strands of a would-be rake's progress; Lauren who was steady and simple and right had brought beauty and security and happiness with her, along with a spectre of possible permanence. Because whatever had seemed to die at the time of Hart's passing seemed to vanish completely when she showed up. No longer could I be as detached as I had been. There was a tension, even distance between us, which made me crave the rebirth of an influence I'd started to mythologize even before we'd heaved packs under the hood of our Beetle, adjusted the valves and gassed up. Still, I was happy with Lauren – happier than I'd been ever, happier than even when wayward and free; because all through that phase I'd had a nagging suspicion, even distrust of… what was it? Hart? Or was it me that I doubted? Familiar, it was in me now as we drove, Curt sleeping and snarfling, her sewing and smiling, me the only one chased by a demon…

The road came to a river, along which we meandered uncountable miles. Over its ripples the lowering sun made deeper gold, reflecting back up into fringe-furred horizons. Evening was coming, dusk of a kind that infects you with old poetry, swirling you into a trance. Only gradually did I become aware of Curtis stretching, 'Nice sunset' groaning, sleep-heavy.

'Yup,' Lauren spoke up. 'Sure is.'

'You nature-trippers mind if I fire a j?' – Beauty requires enhancement.

'I'd do one,' she agreed.

'Ain't gonna put you uptight, man, is it?' – A syrupy sweet scent seeped up into my nostrils.

'I have a choice?' – It wasn't cool to appear paranoid, even if you were driving; so I took my whoosh-whoosh in turn.

'You're so conservative,' Lauren chided.

We were meant to be living on the edge. It wasn't cool to play safe. Still, it was annoying for her to score a point. 'Have a good time, man,' he meanwhile was drawling. 'Stay cool and no one'll give a shit. Like friend Rando says: "Law's a dog: only bites if it kin smell you're afraid."'

Lauren took him literally. 'They'll never change the law; society's not hip enough. We just got to relate to that and make a life for ourselves far, far away.'

'Have a good time, man,' Curtis repeated. 'And don't go all political on us, neither.'

It stopped there. No one was into a high-minded rant. No social theorizing was part of the code too. This was The Big Weekend, and Curt most of all revving up for it.

When Hart and Co. had moved north, he and I had been pretty much the last of the old crowd left down in the City. Then after Lauren had moved in and his bird had flown, Curt had been more or less left on his own. Now boredom is one thing when you have a buddy to share with, but when you don't... Maybe he was stressed about gettin' old too – *quien sabe*? It was hardly cool to mention a thing like that either. Whatever, he was now heading north to *party*! I was too of course, but for him it was, like, urgent to go wild again; to get into whatever new gig those bad northern bros were up to, smash through whatever new barrier Hart had been battering down..

The Beetle crossed a new county line. Darkness was smothering deep indigoes, bridges informing us that we were tracking the Eel, a last leg, stripe of river to lead us into spooky

Eureka. By the side of the highway redwoods climbed the steep hills, screening from view all but narrow strips of lightening stars. Those coastal redwoods, so dense, monumental... near Garberville they broke, and we stopped for gas and so Curt ex's pooch could take a walk in the ferns.

Lauren and I ducked into a shingled tavern abutting the pumps; there a band was warming up, picking out amateur riffs from the latest big-time acid-rock. The place was deserted except for a clutch of fresh-slicked old timers setting to it at the bar. Next to them a hand-lettered sign read, 'Friday Night Blow Out! Come One, Come All (And Bring A Friend!) All You Can Drink & Live Music, $3.00 per'. Smoking and trading a joke with this custom, a country styler pulled pitchers of beer. Between barking laughs and the warm-up picking, the place had a genial air. Twangs formed into boogies – that is, I think they did: the song as it came out sounded familiar but trotted on eccentrically, guitars rippling not wailing like you'd expect, the tune as if filtered through high meadow grasses, rendering it mellow, far from whatever citified, dark incarnation it had originated in...

Lauren rematerialized out of the Ladies. Re-passing the bar, she smiled out a message. I grinned it back at her: yup, we *were* in the north now, and it was good!

One of the old souls on a barstool, rose tattoo down a triceps, doobie hanging from lip, tapped a steel toe in her path while quaffing his beer. 'Get it on, folks!' he hailed as I took her hand in mine and guided her out the flapping doors. 'Friday Night! Show us how it's done!'

His cronies were smiling and the tender cocked a cool eye as she did a twirl for 'em, flaring her skirt, and I lassoed her into the Beetle, coral-hued mane swirling free.

2.

The last leg seemed endless. After forty miles of nothing but redwoods, we crossed a last bridge. To our right forest broke for the river, and we caught sight of a sharp glow of moon in etched crescent. Then we passed into dense obscurity of red-woods again.

Five hours of driving had put me on edge. Expectations ratcheting down from the high of Garberville had ground into a knot of congestion. All of us were nervy, inward, wakeful. The dog whined, shifting, restless. At last the trees broke, and we caught a misty glow of Eureka.

Lanes doubling into freeway sped us past the huge lumber mill marking the south end of town. 'Hey, man,' Curt cleared his throat to drawl, 'you know the way to Hart's place?'

'Naw. Have to ask.'

'May as well stop at a liquor store, pick up a sody.'

Essential to prime yourself for whatever might come…

The freeway declined into a main drag. Traffic lights halted us, despite a near non-existence of traffic. Neon blazed out its message to no one in specific, beckoning us to pull up in front of a long, low-slung storefront, above which pulsated *Liquor*. It was closed. Inside a clock read 10:30 – later than we thought. Gazing up the sidewalk – Friday night, surely something? – we ambled along to the scarlet-signed *Wagon Wheel,* where neon burbled a mug of frothy brew. Breasting swing doors, we stepped into a cement room as non-descript as a hick town bus depot.

One shade-less bulb hung over a pool table; two more dropped Hopper-esque circles of light at each end of a mirrored bar; otherwise, it was the dead of night in there. A small crew of middle-aged men were playing dice as Curt approached the bar-tender, a woman. Lauren and I stretched and peered at old boys like in Garberville, wearing their best Friday night workshirts; but the same zesty spirit was not around. A couple of pool-shooters bumped into the table while missing their strokes with a woozy lack of concern. A cough-dappled laugh hacked out of one corner while from another a tippler, pinning our persons, glared as if Jews had stepped into Mississippi. Turning to his pal, he murmured a word; the pal swivelled to size us up, at which point the barmaid, a garish blonde, having finished with Curt, strolled down the counter to get in on their quip. Placing one hand on each hip, she blessed us with a soundless snort. On this note, tucking one hand through my arm and another through Curt's, Lauren eased us out of there.

Each of us was sucking a bubbly brew as we cruised the dim downtown. Curt tried to relay the barmaid's directions, but for some time we seemed able to do nothing but get lost. Finally we rolled up in front of the right address, and you might have thought we had arrived in another age altogether as well as the far end of this Earth.

Hart's was a lower middle-class, family-sized tract house set on a low slope gazing out over others identical to it. Scattered along avenues drifting down to an invisible ocean, they flickered with glimmers behind thin-curtained windows like a dream on a shore where no sun ever shines. The crescent of moon had been swallowed by mist, like the stars, and you got an impression unlatching his gate and picking your way over untended lawn that you had arrived in some magical wasteland from which you might never return. Curt knocked; no answer. Through shades in the shadows we glimpsed, knocking again; no one. At length sounded a pammer of footfalls, and a tall figure with black hair down to Pendleton-ed pecs opened up.

It was Hart's 6' 6" brother-in-law, Otis.

Ushering us into a living-room, he lowered himself in front of a TV. Curled up at the far end of a horsehair sofa lay a motionless woman. Not a sole other was there.

'Hey Missie, shake it. Curt 'n Jan here.'

The woman looked up and, unravelling like a cat, traded greetings and intros. Lauren covered shyness with a reflection of her yawns. Then we all stood around more or less at a loss, until Missie had coiled back into place.

Otis said hospitably, 'Hey, folks, take a load off!' and set down to rolling a joint.

My body was still travelling, though my mind, jammed with anticipation, had screeled to a halt.

'Everyone else's left,' he explained as we hung there. 'Hart was waitin' for you guys; thought you'd be earlier. Finally went to Strinsky's 'bout an hour ago.'

Curt croaked, 'Where's the party?'

'Hart's b-day y' mean? Tomorrow, after the fair. Lotsa folks.'

He made an effort to give us welcome, but we'd been geared up for so much that his amiable rap seemed like a murmur out of Sleepy Hollow. That suburban quiet only lit by TV and filled otherwise with nothing but us made you gaze out the window to where town and ocean were meant to be and start to lose focus. A sense seemed to pursue us, whistling up in the eaves, that we had reached a last outpost of known civilization.

'Here, man' – Oat lit the j he had rolled and offered it – 'outa sight you're here. Gonna be a craft fair, and *big* party... Big weekend ahead...' Et cet.

We chatted about the drive, reminisced until finally – no more inventory to clear and rush of expectation fully collapsed – I recognized that I was dog-tired. Otis and Missie seemed whacko-ed too. I guess we were all showing it.

'When d'y' think they'll be back?'

'Don' know. Pretty loaded. Mebbe late...'

'Well *I* don't feel like waitin' for those stumblin' bums,' Missie spoke up. 'Beddy-bye for me!'

'For Lauren too, looks like.' – Otis yawned. 'Whe're you folks plannin' to crash?'

I'd assumed Hart would have a room for us. 'We were thinking we'd be welcome here.'

'Yeah? Well... there's an edge of floor over there.'

'Grab a bed while it's goin',' Missie suggested. 'Probably one empty in that room there.'

Curt croaked again, 'Hey, I been waiting six hours to party an' you deadbeats talking about *bed*? And no one else here to get it on with?!'

'Looks like you'll have to keep waitin',' Oat smirked, 'but don't fret. You'll be partying 'til you puke by the time you're done here in the Social Hub of Northern California.'

'Yee-hah,' Missie chorused, 'Brrr!' and, clapping arms around her goose-bumpled nips, repeated, 'Come on, man. Bed!'

8

So they left us dull as cigar-store Indians in that dead-as-a-doornail end of the world. Curt plunked down in front of the TV to light one of the js Oat had rolled. Practised at bevelling the edges of boredom, he engrossed himself in a flurry of snow. So Lauren and I took another of the js and, bidding him goodnight, went to the room Missie had indicated.

Laying our bag down, we crawled in to share a private toke. She curled up against me, resting her head on my arm, puppy-like; and in that moment with all of its rightness all the externals and tensions fled into the warmth of just being there together, alone. We were enveloped. Then she had rolled away and was sighing gently and I hovering nearby, warm and yet wakeful, drifting along in a light, dreamy space... I was in a car again, only this time it was driving as if through plain air, smooth with a faint humming sound. Stars were setting over dark slickened waters, and a crescent of moon glowered between trees in an unearthly light. The air was sharp, cool and, except for the moon and those stars and the thick trees, plus whatever *other* was there silent beside me, I was fully alone now, travelling without memory or consciousness of anything further or live soul and almost unaware of the crash when it came – Footfalls, loud voices, a belt of a laugh... The door swung open and light was lazering through intrusive as a police lamp on my dark desert highway. 'Hey hey, fucker!' a raucous voice cried.

I recognized the jaunty, jovial tone. Straining to deal with invasion of glare, I clapped my lids up and, as if through a strobe-light, saw his face spiral down, a mug of long, drooping moustache and stubbly jaw. Then his body was bouncing on top of our bag, hugging me as I shot up, breath vinous, 'Hey hey, man, how they hangin'? Far fuckin' out!'

I blinked away dazzle and affirmed that, yes – it was Hart.

At first take, he had seemed like some alien pirate, hair longer, streaky, jagged ends falling like epaulets over the seams of a fringed vest. Around his waist snaked a rainbow-hued sash; on his feet were old boots, familiar but more worn-at-heel than on Haight Street many a moon before. The whites of his eyes were red-rimmed, the mouth loose in a grin… Yeah, you could see it was the same old Hart. Only subtly had he changed.

We let off bursts of chuckles, jets of innocuous expletives such as the occasion demanded – that is, he and I did. Lauren, having burrowed herself deeper into the bag, groaned in protest to this rude interruption of her beauty-sleep.

'So that's your ol' lady?' – He laughed merrily. 'Ain't too sociable, huh? Hey little lady, come out! come out! Bring up them peepers an' see your new pal!'

Reluctant, she popped squinting eyes over the lip of the bag. Half of her face grinned a shade of a smile, then slipped back down like an anxious squirrel's. 'Can't you go into the other room, please, if you want to party?'

'So *that's* your new lady?' – Hart chortled some more. 'She's right though, man: party's out there. Get your pants on; way too early for sack.' And clapping me on the back, he exited to rejoin whatever it was he'd swaggered in with.

A low thump of bass pulsating from speakers shook that flimsy tract house like a mild quake. I tried to coax Lauren to get up and join us, but she fended me off with sibling bad vibes. So I pulled on my Levi's like Hart had commanded and ventured out into that transformed space.

The TV was still giving off its dull glare, but the room was now bathed in a purpling black-light. Cousin Randolph, barefooted, kinky hair sprouting, knees and elbows akimbo – uninhibited Rando, ever something of a clown – sat joshing with Curtis and rolling js. Curt himself, full of sniggers, lit each one as it came, puffed it into life and passed it on to a late teenaged girl with straight blonde hair and smooth, opaque skin who sat opposite him against a blank view out the window. Half-reclined in a horsehair armchair, she kicked a crossed leg vaguely to Country Joe and the Fish while gazing sporadically over to a guy in a chair twinned with hers. He had hair nearly white and skin almost albino. Wearing a metallic green letterman's jacket that shone like day-glo in the black-light, he was resting his skull on an antimacassar and drilling eyes on the TV. Their ebony pupils, contrasting ivory lids, held to it like a bird of prey's.

By the door to the kitchen another female was shaking her thang. Bright yellow frizz sprung up off her scalp as if to fly away like a wild maenad's. The way she revolved made this head-dress wave forward, covering her face; but that's not what got your attention. What got your attention – it couldn't help but – strained under the whorl of Cadillac green satin winding down to the floor, enclosing her torso like sausage skin. Stretched nearly to bursting at top, its folds and its flounces plunged toward her navel, cleaving two orbs that might have been stolen off the chest of a double-sized mermaid affixed to the prow of an antique pirate ship. These she rotated in time to the music, suggesting a pre-history in topless dancing.

'Step aside, Vanity,' Hart ordered, swinging in from the kitchen, a gallon of Red Mountain dangling from his index finger.

'Fuck you,' came the answer with admirable nonchalance.

'You got up!' he grinned at me. 'Ol' lady let you?'

A current of joy mixed with irritation at Lauren rose as I fell back under the spell of this inextinguishable presence in my existence. His energy flamed and coursed through the room as he called out, 'Who wants wine?' thrusting his jug in the face of the glassy-eyed blonde.

'Me,' sang the dancer, shimmying up behind him.

'Don't get impatient. You'll get yours in time.'

'Shit,' Vanity spat. 'I'm dry!'

'Stay that way,' quipped Randy, 'an' you won't git in trouble…' Licking a fresh j, he held it out. 'Here, suck on this.'

She brushed it aside. He sniggered, a reaction evoking guffaws from Curt. Yet even if her hauteur did seem a bit overdone, Vanity held their focus. She emanated a power she knew all about, Vanity. I recalled having heard of her down in the City but hadn't laid eyes on her 'til now. She was one of those real-life characters you rarely run into but hear so much of you think you have. Vanity… Curt tracked her motions, salivating. *He* recalled: insatiable Vanity, the great challenge, love witch.

I guzzled red and, settling by him on the sofa, reminisced. Puffing more js, we eyed her and chortled. Nodding our heads, we watched as guitar riffs drooled their acid odysseys down four picture-less walls. Up went our spirits, into that excitable dampness that always enwombed you when in Hart's place. He himself had crossed to sit on an arm of the chair holding the underage blonde. Randy's toke being potent, airy, stupefying, our gazes followed amid stuttering laughs. Obbligatos of electronic leads or single words in a lyric superimposed images over the distant, semi-abstract aura of whatever was going on, or seemed to be, in his contorting features. Hart and the girl… I began to think that he wouldn't get his way with her; that his riffs were deforming; that something else was precious, even sacred in her epistemology. His presence seemed like no more than smoke off a flame to her. She'd maybe smile, drop the odd monosyllable, nod but remain secured to this *other* unknown, as if alien god. He'd offer her tokes, spool out his best lines, chide her for not 'gettin' it on', but she'd just revolve those dead blues and grin absently, as if some esoteric knowledge put her on a plane high above him. Now and again her gaze would veer off to the albino and seem to recharge off the sphinx-like stare he still riveted on the TV, as if some mild, euphoric message were coming out of it, from Neverland. It was entrancing, but Hart seemed unnerved by it, or at least driven into more boisterousness – more than us even, which is saying a lot. Curt was now way under the spell of Vanity, taunting her motions with a salacity of grins, a gutterality of quips, inciting the jug-jug of flesh by pulling bigger and better bills out of his wallet, trying to get her to peel that sausage skin down. Beside him Randolph, having two now to josh at, bantered away like a game-show host, g-ing them up, overtopping each witty quip with an afterthought that led to two more. Vanity for her part just kept gyrating, every impertinence moving her to thrust her chin higher, whirl her frizz wider or snort more contemptuously, 'Forget it, man; you can do better than that!' Her responses might have made you think she was repelled, if her performance had not been in flat contradiction of it. The brute sensuality fattened on lubricious insult made it hard for me not to be drawn into my own seepage of lust for her; and as Randy sniped and Curtis slurped, I found myself swirling down into mustier currents, so that it was only gradually that I began to refocus on Hart and *his* problem, this being when or because – some signal having passed between them – the blonde and albino rose in mute syncopation and, as if levitating, drifted between us and Vanity out through the swinging door to the kitchen.

Like a bird-of-prey, Vanity swooped. 'Is Harty upset? Hey babe, serves you right!' And she danced with more vehemence, as if satisfied, bringing a sticky silence down on the rest of us.

Even Randy went hushed as, eyes travelling to Hart, we watched chagrin struggle up to belch its way out over the electronic goop dripping down the dun walls onto horse-hair.

'Fucking smack-heads,' he muttered.

I guess that was it. Because when the pair re-emerged, eyes glowing more than ever, though with a glassiness that now seemed paralytic, green and gold of the letterman's jacket luminous as neon, the albino mouthed in a far-away lilt at our host, 'Hey man, gonna split, 'k? Thanks a bunch.'

They passed on to exit, the blonde revolving eyes back and voicing a distant 'Bye' Hart's direction; to which, up through anger, he could only emit an ironic, 'Adios.'

Bang. Exeunt.

The screen door bounced and, while Hart hung there rueful, I had for the first time a sense of this Achilles of our hot youth in defeat. O, you could remember times when his riffs hadn't worked or his prancing style dissipated into a laughing fecklessness, but I couldn't recall one when it had seemed to affect him, 'til now. There he stood staring into the blank space they'd vacated, mouth pursed, forehead grinced. 'Come on!' Vanity crowed in derision at him like a portent, shaking her thing. 'Hey lover-boy, do the dirty with me!'

She was hooting this as he repeated, half in a mutter at nowhere, at us, 'Fucking smack-heads', trying to rationalize it.

'Sure as hell better not've been shooting up in my place...'

'Forget it! Forget everything, babe!' she cooed through the thick air, intent on nothing but coaxing his eyes back to her; because Vanity had no shred of interest in anything else in that place – *he* was her dark prince, all that she wanted. And flashing a look into him basilisk-like, she beckoned, sashaying up and limbo-ing off in a new fury of motion, warbling in sing-song, 'Forget it, go get it, baby-boy. Be happy with me!'

In a sudden lurch, he tossed back two inches of red and, bleary eyes pinning her as if unsure who she was, called out ''s late!' – You could see she would get him. 'Far out you guys're here', he nodded at us. 'Picked out your spots yet to sleep?'

I nodded yes. Curt was sullen: he'd been nursing an idea that *he*'d be one to peel that sausage-skin down.

'Far out,' Hart repeated, and draining the last of his vial – 'Bed for me now. See you fucks in the a.m.' At which point, the love-witch trailing in triumph, he exited too.

3.

Grey light roused me early. My head felt like a bruise. Beside me Lauren slept in child-like silence. Tossing around for what seemed hours, I felt sticky and ill in that heavy, crowded bag. Just as I was realizing you couldn't live in the land of nod forever, her body had curled itself around mine and a gentle hand was rubbing my thigh.

'Some night, huh?'

I made a noise.

'You oughtta groan... I thought you guys'd never quit.'

It made me cross. She was right of course, but it sounded so preachy. Especially in Hart's house, the code was ever to *get it on*.

I hid my crossness under my hangover. She said no more, and irritation faded into remorse. Getting up, she put on a pair of blue-and-white striped slacks that clung to her bones, making her seem almost frail. Over her head she pulled a Mexican wedding shirt with pastel stitches up front. Eying me sideways, she brushed out her hair, all that strawberry gold. I rolled my face in the pillow away from dull glare seeping around a flimsy shade. But there was no use trying to stay buried. So I got up, braving dizziness, and stepped over to lay palms on her temples.

We hovered there nuzzlingly. The skin around her eyelids puffed out. 'I didn't sleep very well either,' she breathed.

I held her tight, stretching my muscles and drawing strength out of her billowy tenderness. Trying to squeeze off our worries, she hugged me back with a pressure that seemed to apologize and plead for things to be right at the same time. Feeling appeased, and ashamed, I pulled on my Levi's.

Through the living-room windows more opaque light seeped in from the northern day. At a distance you could just make out a grey, chilly Pacific beyond modest stucco. Oat and Missie sat on the sofa slurping coffee and perusing the morning paper.

'Look who's decided to get up,' he riffed.

'Some night last night.' – I flopped onto horsehair.

'That's what Hart said.'

'He up yet?'

'Tapped at his door to see if he wanted to go t' the fair. Not too thrilled at bein' interrupted.'

'That figures,' said Lauren, who was gazing into the yard to where a golden-haired tot tossed a stick for Curt's ex's canine.

'Told us to go on without 'im, be down later.'

'What a pretty girl!' she said.

Missie looked up from the Calendar section of the *Chron*. 'Not in the street, are they?'

'Such a beautiful kid. Is she yours?'

'Yup.' – Missie returned to reading. 'And all the sleepless nights that go with it…'

'You two still interested in the fair?' Oat asked over this. 'If so, we oughtta get shakin'.'

'I guess. Curt asleep too?'

'In there, him and Rando. Don't worry 'bout them, though; out for the count.'

So we climbed into Otis's battered VW bus and drove down to the centre of town. Low houses passed interspersed here and there with telephone poles or eucalypti or palm trees that had strayed too far north. Now and then he would point out some sight he figured to be of interest; the place really did look like a slough of despond in grey day, but this didn't seem to faze him as he ruminated in good-neighbourly fashion. Close to the main drag a handful of Victorians rose out of the normalcy of stucco one-storeys; weather-worn detail and archaic garrets gave them a poignant, bygone aura. Beyond overgrown lawns, one had been decorated with a fresh coat of pink, making it seem nearly frisky; that, he explained, was where the commune that sponsored the Crafts Fair was making its headquarters.

On we whirred through an even grid of streets and pulled up perpendicular to the main drag. Across the way in a vacant lot folks were laying out merchandise. Smack in the middle of hardware shops, five-and-dimes, surplus clothing stores, cafeterias and so on, it seemed an unlikely spot for revealing and celebrating a counter-culture, but it was the sole place in town which the commune had been allowed to rent, Oat explained. Over to it we sauntered, into handmade wooden booths displaying oaken carvings, metal-work, ceramic pots, beaded jewellery, tooled leather, stitched vests and a plethora of other less nameable items in a myriad of shapes, colours and sizes. Less professional folk who could not afford booths were arranging their stuff on benches or makeshift tables. Upwards of forty different stands encircled a central platform studded with speakers and microphones, portending future events. Good country souls milled around: bearded mountain guys with scrubbed, ruddy women smiling in appreciative benignity; braided mamas carrying babes like papooses or holding the gripped paw of some new initiate into the venture of walking. A musician with downy sideburns tested his skill on a flute tooled from bamboo while its maker trilled descant on a similarly-sculpted recorder. A lass reached deep in the folds of her ground-dusting skirt to find cash to pay for a fringed leather purse, while a middle-aged guru in lotus position held a group spellbound as he grooved the sounding-board of a balsa-wood lute to inlay with rosewood striations.

A festival atmosphere reigned. Otis and Missie's child picked it up and ran with it; Lauren, following, glowed it back at me infectiously. She would become a little kid here too, the look said, where time stopped or contrived to deny forward motion. Because everything here seemed to conjure the past – early California past, pioneer days, lost Injun eras. There were heavy scents on the air – of incense, freshly-baked bread, sensemilla. A faint jingling as of beads or of tiny bells sounded, possibly wind-mobiles; and after a spell everything seemed to hark back further, beyond our American past, to evoke county fairs in a Celtic north of England, medieval bazaars in central Europe, congregations less specific in times more pristine, remote. Ahead of me Oat, Missie and Lauren chawed while the girl-child, having bought a balloon, whirled as satellite to their progress. The women laughed as Oat caught her to hoist on a shoulder; meanwhile, I lagged back to slip deeper into reveries of my own... So this was the future, this evocation of smiling pasts, this guileless brotherhood of craft. So this was why the many had beat out their exile, taking their treks to discover a more fundamental and, for them, relevant lifestyle. They had returned to the land to grow their own food, school their hands in more venerable arts, develop self-knowledge and sufficiency, raise their children outside the given norm. And here on festival day they had migrated in from their cabins and tee-pees, wood-stoves and coal fires, to lay out their creations and admire those of others – so much like the past, so foreign to our brash present...

At the edge of their encampment, over by the main drag, middle-aged men lurked in tight groups, joking and raising short billed caps from their pates, scratching flecks of dandruff from close-cropped hair, pinning the scene. What rancour or pleasure passed through *their* minds? what ghosts of Saturdays gone when they had been young? what glimpses of times when they'd had jobs good enough to throw away half a week's wages on a weekend like this? What nagging fears of the future plagued *them*, these ex-working-stiffs sipping Bud out of brown bags and spatting glops of chewing-tobacco on the sidewalk? Women with wrinkled foreheads and in horn-rimmed spectacles, wearing pointy-toed sneakers beneath puce pedal-pushers, hurried past to get groceries or return laden with bags, dragging conventional kids behind, curious to stare at these aliens in their midst. To them as to us, the Craft Fair suggested, 'We are self-contained and resourceful, energetic and happy. Are we not the chosen ones of a New Dawn?' To which seemed to come in a chorus of para-religious certitude, *yes*! And only when a gang of teenagers in flat-tops and greased fenders, cigarettes drooping from lips à la James Dean, cruised by in a garish, low-riding Chevette, engine roaring seven g's and tires laying rubber, did this version of the future seem at all challenged.

Lauren rushed back to me with a flurry of observations, wanting me to check out this dressmaker, that wood-carver *et cet*. I told her I was content just to drift, nursing my head, and she flounced off disappointed. So festival day continued to swirl around me; and partly enthralled, partly sceptical, still hangdog, I tracked the good folk as they slid by like incarnate ghosts. Clocking a pride of young hipsters hanging out on a kerb, I saw them cool-grin one another while trading a covert j. Two chicks ambled by barely raising their moccasins off skit-scatting gravel, their long hair swaying and wide eyes revolving to take in the looks of trepidatious interest. Both were dressed in a uniform of jeans and loose blouses, beneath which their round pretties bounced braless and free. They seemed to float above purpose, only now and then responding to a passing stare as if with a rippling half-laugh. Crossing between me and the would-be hip youths, one rolled a cerulean orb my direction, returning my gaze as if not fully conscious, and I realized she was the blonde who'd ditched Hart the night before to get high, or low or whatever it was with the albino in green letterman's jacket.

On a corner by the main drag scruffy Rando had surfaced. Towering above the hip kids, he had brushed frizz from an eye and was proceeding to rap. Pulling myself together, I started over, but before I could get to him I was caught by Curt, who came weaving toward me with Hart just behind – a pair of bleary-eyed pirates in tie-dye.

'Far out, man,' Hart grinned, shaking, revving himself up for new day. 'Here you are, fucker.' – Fishing a pack of 'grettes from my pocket, he helped himself.

'Happy b-day,' I said.

He smirked at Curtis, who cadged a smoke too.

'Should we tell 'im?'

'Up to you,' Curtis played.

'He may be too good a buddy to jive.'

'Tell me what?' I asked, nettled.

Hart's grin became wry. 'Don't let anyone know, man, but it ain't my b-day for real. Just an excuse to get these honky-tonk lard-asses giggin'.'

'Sheet!' – We chortled as if into some righteous prank.

'What a scene,' he went on, nervier still, and we stood around blowing smoke rings as folks passed saying 'Howdy', him tapping a boot heel and flicking Captain Hook locks until it began to seem that, despite appearing to know and be known by everyone and his brother, he wasn't entirely at home here. 'Way too early, man. Gotta get loose… You seen Oat?'

So I found myself leading them through the booths and the barkers to locate our crew. Hart paid scant attention to wares on display, only glanced around now and then with quick, hawk-like turns of the head. 'Hey ho, fucker!' he hooted once we'd found Oat, Missie and Co by the bandstand where amps were being switched on. 'Let's get in your bus and get loaded. Scene's way too heavy on an empty head.'

Good-natured Oat was ready to oblige, but Missie complained, 'You guys… always wanting to get loaded!' which made him hesitate. 'You wanna go right now, or – ?'

'Yo,' Hart insisted. 'I ain't takin' these craft-fuckers cold.'

So we turned and set out for where Oat's bus was parked.

'Where're you going?' Lauren asked, pattering up behind.

'T' get high,' I murmured uneagerly. 'Wanna come?'

She looked to the others and saw Men Only. 'I'll stay with them,' she said, of Missie and child. 'Come back soon, 'K?'

'Ol' ladies!' Curt disparaged as we headed on.

'Gonna be as whipped as Oat soon, pal,' Hart sniggered.

'Fuck you,' Otis and I grunted in unison, and the two hungover pirates hooted as if they'd scored a direct hit.

We picked up Randy en route along with some dude in dark, greasy locks and a low-rider's leathers, and into the back of Otis' VW camper we climbed. Randy chid us for being dead-beat – 'Gotta loosen up, kids, ain't time for sourpusses like in bad need of a night's sleep. Hart, you just rose out of the graveyard or what? I been goin' a week now, haven't begun to fight; give me that thang...' and grabbing a j, he brushed frizz from an eye to suck on it. Oat pulled a curtain against the exterior world and, marijuana fug gathering, we were sealed in. Even so, it was hard not to feel paranoid – so many rednecks out there – nor did the greaser beside me evoke any sense of safety. But neither he nor the venue seemed to faze Otis, who sniggered at Randy, or Curtis, who rolled j after j. Only Hart seemed as jumpy as I was, though that was out of a different anxiety. Swallowing nerves, I puffed along with them while Randy continued his tale of week-long revels. If this was meant to conjure a fair mood, it succeeded to a degree that, by the time three js had passed and his bloodshot squint was fixed as if in eternal mirth, we appeared to be floating on top of a general soup of bonhomie. Then Hart said, 'Hey frizz-head, you just talk too much sometimes, like just repeat the same fuckin' record.' To which Randy went 'Me?' pretending high dudgeon, though winking at us. To which Hart mused, shifting topic, 'I wonder if that chick'll be here today...'

'I saw her a while back,' I said, knowing who he meant.

'Still not loose enough... Hey Rando, how 'bout a stumbler.'

'You got stumblers?' Oat echoed.

'Might say I had a few,' Randy drawled and out of his work-shirt pocket pulled a baggy of red capsules that looked like jelly-beans. 'Almost forgot; glad you reminded. Now don't get grabby – y'all get a share, then we best get down to business...'

This last phrase was put to the greaser, who added no word. Meanwhile, Randy dispensed one capsule each of Seconal to Otis, Hart and Curtis. 'I shouldn't,' Oat said as he took his, 'but it's Hart's b-day, so…' Grinning, he swallowed.

When my turn came, I hesitated.

'What's up with you, man?' Hart challenged.

'Nothin'. I'm just savin' for tonight. Give me a fifth of J Daniels, an' I'll be cooking!'

'Right on,' Randy crooned. 'Every man to his poison!'

But Hart wasn't pleased. 'Better eat one,' he admonished.

'Hart boy,' Randy countered, 'don't be givin' my stash if'n the kid don't want it. Got his mind on firewater; 'sides, the less I give, the more I have to do business with.'

I was as irked at Hart as he evidently was with me but Randolph, playing the genial m-c, managed to get us back into groove – or maybe not quite. Because shortly our prince of pirates was voicing my feeling that we ought to be paranoid about staying in that bus any longer.

'Only get bit if you smell scared,' Randy quipped, but Hart had slid the door back and was stepping out. Oat, Curt and I following left only frizz-head in that aromatic compartment with the greaser, to conduct such 'business' as they had.

Hart grinned at us behind him. So was that all he needed? some display to re-affirm his status as leader? – Drilling bleary eyes into mine, he seemed to want to know if it was OK: if despite time and distance I was still under the spell. And you know what? All my annoyance seemed to melt in the heat of that gaze. There was real warmth there, it said; real worth in the fact of our bonding. So again I was caught up and ready to be renewed; to be corralled in that aura of lusty excitement that always seemed to surround you when in Hart's space.

He'd draped an arm over my shoulder. 'Sure good to have you with us, little bud…' Then as if suddenly realizing we were in the thick of a crowd, he dropped this too-overt sign of affection and, shaking himself loose, resumed his pose of checking and being checked out by every styler that passed. So I felt us drift apart again. It was as if all you could hope for out of fellow-ship with him was to rise to the crest of a wave only to tumble back down its face into darkness and whirlpool.

Shivering, I hid the fact under a surface of camaraderie. And mercifully, sights and smells and noises were reasserting their aura before we'd gone many steps on. Twangy guitar riffs running over and around one another led us up to where the band was now setting to it on the platform.

'Far out,' I ventured, 'they're gettin' it on!'

'Yeehaw,' Otis muttered as we rejoined the gals, planted on their bottoms to a redwood log in front of the stage.

The band had begun jangling into a tune. Now it was cantering up to full stride. In my marijuana-fugged mind the notes came out sharp, fluid, nearly hypnotizing. Lauren slipped a hand through a crook of my arm and squeezed close; she started to say something, but I ssshed – 'Hey, don't talk now, just listen!' – so she went sad. I kissed her, but you could see in a blink that we would diverge too, though the sounds of the separate instruments were simultaneously merging, weaving a fabric out of which you might pick a hundred luminous strands... Acoustic rhythm lay down basic chords in a quick, full-bodied strum, while under them bass pounded out component notes at a jostling, travelling pace. On the drums forward motion split into small, slightly nerve-janging fragments while over all slid the mellow, mercurial riffs of a pedalled-steel guitar. A fiddler began trading off bowing descant with singing in low, down-home twang, and in this way the music pulled you up in its saddle. Eyes passed from stage to a louring sky, then dropped back to focus on not quite either so much as some object in a vague distance, which seemed solid and happy, transcendent and hyper real at the same time. A jug of wine passed from deep in the crowd up to Missie and Oat, then to Lauren and me; I turned to pass it to Curtis and Hart, but they had dematerialized, dissolving as if back into anonymous benignity. So it passed on through bodies while up on stage the fiddler announced a new song that was special, and the lead guitar player joined in to intone harmony over a countrified rap, and at the refrain their respective instruments rode over the vocals, trading the lead, reflecting and mutating each other's riffs until both had melded, forming an incongruous grid out of what had seemed semi-conflict. The rhythm guy took up playing bottle-neck under, and joyous, unbroken moaning slid back and forth until, somehow, the disparate, contradictory nature of country blues with its unassuming, confident, homespun motifs and hard rock with its sexy, lurid, aggressive keening had fused into a new whole. The electric lead fizzled into narcotic passivity while fiddle notes capered up on tippy-toe; then liquid sounds rose to swell and gush out, washing those guttural fiddle-bowings clean away. For a moment it seemed as if some miracle was at hand, some ultimate synthesis, and we marvelled. Filled with tingling envy, I squeezed Lauren's hand where it lodged between my elbow and arm. We were together again at last, closing in on the All, free of all apprehensions, moving in on the One, Everlasting, Forever. We were in the north truly, and it *was* good. And so it would be until, in the midst of rapture, the rollicking, headlong impulse was snapped by a string flying off the face of the lead axe, making a wail shrill and mournful and stopping all sonic motion. Thereupon, inevitably, the band had to announce a break.

Everyone was drifting down out of separate heavens as a mountain man with straw hair and a haystack of beard climbed onto the platform to take the mike. 'Brothers and sisters,' he intoned sonorously, baggy overalls held up by red suspenders under the tails of a Pendleton shirt. 'Brothers and sisters...' The afternoon wearing down... 'Brothers and sisters...' An unsunned sky seeming to go heavier, darker... 'My brothers and sisters...' It felt like it was going to rain.

'Wanna split?' Oat asked, stifling a yawn.

'Brothers and sisters...' the voice rumbled.

'Wanna go?' I asked Lauren.

The yawn spread to her too. 'Sure,' she said meekly.

So we cut through the crowd where benign faces were lifted up as if towards the light – a light that seemed half-existent as their mountain guy took on revivalist mode.

'That's Michael,' Oat offered.

'Who?'

'Guy who organized the commune, that did the Fair.'

'Ah.'

Lethargic, we made our way on to the bus. Beyond the good folk, you could just make out Hart's peaky features and jagged locks as he hung on a corner jigging a boot-heel, smoking and rapping into the dead eyes of the blonde.

'Fucking smack-freaks,' I thought. 'Well, he's found her. Hope he's loose…'

At a far corner we came upon Randy and Curtis, the former witticizing in vintage fashion. 'There you folks are! look like a funeral. Why the long faces?'

'Beat.'

'Shit, I been cookin' six days an' hardly begun… Run along now, get yer beauty sleep; gotta be pert for the party. Don' worry 'bout us here, be along in good time…' And brushing furze from an eye, he winked as we passed as if he had found the secret of how to live in this world, which maybe in that moment he had.

Oat's battered bus sped up a hill dotted with domiciles stuc-co-ed low to the ground. In front of Hart's place he pulled to the kerb and Missie called 'See y' tonight, kids' as they let us out and smoothed off like the 'rents dropping tots off at school.

Curt's ex's Lab pawed at the door to get free as we came across the weedy lawn. Otherwise, we were like the sole living creatures at that lonesome end of the world.

We shut ourselves in the bedroom and pulled down the shade against a gun-metal sky. 'Ooo I've missed you today,' Lauren cooed, winding her warmth around me.

'Don't speak,' I murmured, and sensually burned.

'You mad?' she pondered, pulling away.

'Nah. Should I be?'

'I don't know. You seemed distant…'

'Sorry,' I breathed, drawing her close. 'I'm not mad at you at all now, 'K?'

She nuzzled up, and I squeezed and kissed her, and slowly began to undress her. She smiled with eyes crinkling up like a child's; and then I was with her again fully, feeling her soft places and wondering how I'd let it all slip away. We were together again now, her pale skin and smooth mounds and soft, feathery parts hard against me, and me hungry for them. Our nakedness meshed, soft and then hard, violent, then silent, screaming as if, then gentling back and forth in and out of bliss and sweet pain.

4.

A knock on the door brought us out of vague sleep. It was dark as a crow's wing, and in the slipstream of dreams you could think it was the dead of night.

The knock came again. 'Yo?' I muttered.

A female silhouette stretched over a rhombus of light. 'You folks might shake a leg. Things oughtta be gettin' on pretty soon. Food in the kitchen 'f you're hungry.'

Silhouette and light withdrawing, the door closed.

I twisted in darkness, unable to rise.

'Who was that?' Lauren wondered.

'Vanity.'

'Who's Vanity?'

'Hart's ol' lady, I guess.'

'She sure has a swamp-full of frog in her throat.'

The voice *was* raspier than the night before, and incongruous in its housewifely message.

Lauren got up and raised the shade with a snap. Last embers of day turned her skin a will o' the wisp white. I had a flash of Vanity's cleavage, which morphed into memory of loose-fitting tops on the blondes, and Lauren's flesh went thrill-less, almost like the ectoplasm of a ghost. Eager to move on to whatever was new in excitement, I went too fast. Before long she was out of bed again and pulling on a calico dress she'd hand-sewn.

It was pretty and right in a homespun sort of way, but...

'Have I blown it again?' she wondered.

'Course not,' I bluffed, but you couldn't fool her.

She brought tears to her eyes, making me feel guilty in spades. Those pale blues gleaming, she was so precious and sweet that I could only resolve never ever to hurt her again. Getting up, I went over and wrapped her up tight in my arms. Gradually she gave way, and we rocked soft as babes.

'OK?' I asked, kissing her lids.

'I hoped you'd like it... I really did.' She wiped wet from her cheeks and gazed down over the lacy stuff which covered her hummocks of breast. 'It just feels like me now...' Her voice had gone small, like a vulnerable kid's.

After kissing me back, she turned to combing her hair, and I got dressed. What could you do but love her?

Hart's house was filling with folks straggling back from the fair. In the kitchen women were dishing out corn-on-the-cob and meat stew. A hearty sense of the past had invaded, echoing thanksgiving feasts and pioneer hoe-downs. We took our plates and put them on our knees in the packed living-room, where good neighbourly spirits hovered around.

People were strewn on the floor Injun-style, chawing about what they'd seen in the day. In one corner a bearded bro' plucked an acoustic guitar, then experimented with his knife to see if he could get bottleneck sounds by pressing strings to the frets. Next to him another guy tapped out rhythm on a plate as if it were a bongo drum. Some went silent to absorb these vibrations; others continued to chew their cud in quiet, amiable tones. Out came the toke, and one or two started to spin off into phantasms or into dreaming awake.

Vanity, subdued, seemed a stranger in this company. Pacing in front of the kitchen, she held two hands on one hip and pinned the proceedings as if presiding madam. Hair pulled back severe, she showed for the first time the howl in the bones of her cheeks. Circles beneath thyroidic eyes made it seem as if she'd been weeping all day. Cigarettes puffed end-to-end punctuated lioness steps as she waited impatient for something to happen.

Against this the rational, militantly humble spirit of the counter-culture seemed too good by contrast, un-vital.

Lauren brought out the moccasins she'd been stitching in the car. See, she showed me, they're almost finished! She fit in so well, settled there listening in mild half-attention to the rustic pit-pat. She was so good, so like *them*, that I started to split off again, impatient like Vanity for something more to happen, something wild or risk-taking, indecent. Watching her pace with those big berthas out, I lost myself in whatever it was she seemed to embody. For a spell she became *my* fantasy, chasing all others, not least those wrapped up in Lauren. At last, as in answer to our fretful hopes, all calm was broken by a brash, hooting entrance of Hart, Curt and a half dozen other Dionysiacs, eyes dazzled from booze and reds, huzzahing to *party*.

'Hey hey, you fuckers! Let's get it on!'

Like a band of buccaneers arriving on shore, they laughed and they jigged, threw out mindless quips, swirled around agitating the mass of *good* folk to synthetic exuberance.

Dragging a keg in, they set it up in the kitchen. Dancing in front of all, Hart handed out fresh js while Curt surfaced before me to slide a pint of JD up out of a brown bag.

'Courtesy, Randolph. Told me to tell you that business is booming an' by the time he gets here he 'spects you to be finished with this an' ready for another.'

Lauren watched me glug a maiden sip. 'You aren't going to drink the whole thing, are you?' – I grinned at Curt, who produced an identical bottle out of an identical brown bag to clink against mine. 'I don't believe you guys!'

We let out a brotherly *yeehaw*.

'Randy says we gotta have *everything* here in the north,' Curtis brayed. 'Ain't havin' no strangers claimin' him as a friend hangin' out on his turf po-faced.'

'We'll show these bumpkins how it's done!' I *macho*-ed back.

'Yay-hey!' Curt emitted, and we guzzled a gullet-full more as a wave of others washed in, including Michael, the leader, and remnants of the commune.

Around them the good people gathered like filings to a magnet. Meanwhile Vanity, hands on hip still, stayed at her post by the kitchen, eying all in shrewd scepticism. At least *her* crowd was coming now, her hipsters, her Hart. Only with them could she loosen like she felt, exhibit as she wanted, freak out if it pleased her, and the clean-livers could accept it or jump in a frigid Pacific for all she could care. Her thyroidic orbs followed him, prince of pirates, raucously prancing, grinningly pushing maryjane through the lips of the American Gothic. Yet even Hart danced more decorously in the precincts of Michael. Out of some political correctness before the fact, he seemed to feel need to pay obeisance to this chief of the counter-realm, moral Hart. But Vanity knew who the real Hart was. She knew he courted these gentle folk only to get 'em to join in, add to his performance, reinforce his ever-hungry hostly pride. Because the real Hart was her wild one, even if he hadn't yet revved it up to a pitch so that the crafties couldn't field back his banter in their benignly head-wagging, bovinely easy way.

Wild Hart. Or wasn't he truly so wild anymore? Weren't there younger ones coming, going farther in risk, and didn't he know it? Did he fear it? Did he rue growing old? Could he do so with grace? What future was there, an inner voice might ask: youth is the season you were made for, even to the point of being master of it. Youth is the time when the Harts of our lives shine like gods or the sun, so how could this one cope with the prospect of age? wild Hart, hero of our yesterdays?

What *would* happen to him now, coming down the years? – Vanity watched as he danced his spirit over all, or tried to. She loved him in her way, you could see: loved him enough to be jealous to have him for herself, the glare said, radiating contempt for the normals he blessed. It seemed to dare him to look back at her, which she knew he would in his sweet time. Stuffing a j in her lips as through the others, he would produce his own brown bag to uncover a slim flask of the red Ripple he knew she favoured, and in that moment she would triumph. Then he'd be off again, dancing his way into the mass, turning the sound up to pulse-stressing levels while more pretty and/or musty bodies came tumbling in through his door.

A dispute over music. The guitar guy in the corner and plate bongo-drummer packed up their percussives as electric rock began to drool down the bare walls.

Lauren beside me kept sewing moccasins, but my throat was burning from too many swallows, so I said, 'Hey, put those things away. Let's have us a time!'

'But I'm almost finished!'

I could hardly disguise my disdain.

'All right,' she snipped and, exiting to the bedroom, made me feel our separation in spades. Inflamed by the spirit of *party*, how could I see her as other than a ball-n-chain?

Coming back, she re-settled beside me with a look mixed of anger and plea. Then Hart was hanging over us, loose-mouthed, sticking a j through her lips, forcing them into a smile. Cringing, she held back a fall of red hair to take a light from the match he struck in a lewd sweep off the seat of his jeans. Somehow he knew how things were between us.

'Don't pay attention to this asshole, Lauren; he's never as right as he thinks he is!' – Her face brightened and, dropping an arm down over her shoulder, he added in my direction, 'She's all right, your lady. Maybe a little uptight, but…' Pinching one of her nipples, he made her squeal; then he was off again in one of his rude dances of mirth.

Another wave of folk washed in, the dead-eyed blonde among them, along with her lookalike friend. Both wore fixed grins as they checked out the scene; spotting them, Hart was off like dog to a bone. The albino with paralytic stare slipped in as if unseen behind them and went off to his corner to rivet tight, ebony eyes on the crowd, gold and green of his letterman's jacket sheening as if an electric current was coursing through it.

The party ratcheted up, 'Purple Haze' wailing, hoarse voices competing. Whatever tension there was between groups seemed to suspend itself so that chit-chat could pass, sodas get guzzled and eyes take up squinting through a proud maryjane haze drifting up to the plasterboard ceiling. From her corner Vanity, mammaries bulging, continued to glower while sipping her syrupy red. Curt salivated at her, but she affected not to see. Then Missie surfaced in front of us bright-eyed.

'O hi!' – Lauren lightened: a new friend, she hoped.

Otis ambled up, droop-jawed.

'Took your time,' I put to him.

'Had to work forever to get him up,' Missie jibed. 'I tell him not to hang around Randy when he's into stumblers, but… Frailty thy name is menfolk.'

Otis ignored this. 'Got your firewater?' he put to me.

'Workin' on it. You want some?'

'Too potent for my blood.'

So we hung there, action swirling around us, though the buzz Hart had brought in had begun to fade as he settled down by the side of the zombie blondes.

Curtis reeled over, sucking his pint. 'Got ya beat!' he said holding it up against mine.

'Not for long.' – I chugged enough to make a dipso dizzy.

'Y' guys're nuts,' Otis smirked. 'Satisfied with our northern partyin' yet, ho-dad?'

Curt revolved a leer back to Vanity. 'Mebbe…'

'Where's Rando.' Oat went on. 'You juice-heads seen 'im?'

We allowed as we hadn't. 'Fuck Randy and his reds!' Missie meanwhile protested and, peeling off from her husband, transported herself into a gaggle of crafties.

Full of liquor, I re-flopped on the sofa by Lauren. She slipped a hand through my arm. 'Sip?' she inquired, eying me obliquely, friction between us having apparently wandered off again. 'Sorry,' she added. 'I haven't been much fun…'

She was so warm then. ''s OK. I been pretty mean…' And with a sense of my capacity to hurt her heavy on me, I pulled her chin around and kissed her.

She went radiant.

Hart's b-day revving roared up into another gear. Curt was hanging at Vanity's side, watching her guzzle, coaxing her to perform. He'd whisper some ribaldry; she'd throw her head back and shimmy at him, wagging those gargantuas into his face; and again I felt errant urges. Fantasy burbling swirled into lust for some rash, orgiastic state of being, and Lauren once more fled from my soul like a shadow flitting out of a mirror.

On went the swirling, taking Hart from the blonde to the nucleus around Michael. He hung there ten seconds, then meandered back to us. A beat held him over our heads, grinning down, drooping a hand on my shoulder, sighing as if weighed low with cares. He murmured again how happy he was we'd made it up to his place, but before you could answer he was off, heading back to the nimbus around Ms Dead-Eyes.

Missie resurfaced to rap with Lauren. Taking the chance as given, I stirred my stumps and went over to where Hart was now haranguing the blonde and her friend about smack and why you shouldn't do it. They nodded knowingly, half-grinning as if from a great height, a reaction so cool that it made his drunken riff seem absurd, so I said, 'Hey man, 's too heavy; here, have a swig', which caught him mid-sentence, tossing him off stride. But he recouped balance and, clamping my neck in a vise, grabbed my pint and continued for his audience, 'Now here's a sensible dude: won't even chew a stumbler to get loose but already's fried half his brains on JD!' which allowed the cool chickies to train their gaze down on *me* from on high, earning Hart a self-consoling hoot, after which he set back into his intruded-on rap. So I was off again, repeating 'Too heavy!' this time to Otis, who, forehead wrinkled and hand to the chin, stood in a corner deep in rumination with the authoritative Michael.

'Ready to puke, gremmie?' Oat smirked, but I was off yet again, weaving now toward the kitchen in whose flapping door-way loomed Vanity and Curt.

'Hey haw,' Curtis croaked. 'Let's get this lard-ass gig goin'!'

Clinking bottle to bottle, we swigged at our dregs.

'Hey man, check this out,' he added, nudging me to the bathroom, and opened its door on a naked barrel of a man with two dimple-assed gals towelling ruddy cheeks as turgid water swirled down around a rusted drain.

'C'mon in,' the mountain guy crooned as if a hospitable *maître d'*. 'Take the grit off. Plenty a room for all.'

Slamming the door in his face, Curt yowled as if on a frat panty-raid. Whereupon a light seemed to flick on in a drink-sodden brain – *why not?* why not string the whole get-it-on ethos out to its logical conclusion?

'The hell with these organic food nudies!' he cried. 'Let's show these northern dip-danglers how to *really* party!'

Crowing in old-time brotherly fashion, we chorused 'Alright!' clinking our empties and toasting the holy words, 'Liberate yourselves, motherfuckers!'

Reverting to Vanity, Curt threw over a shoulder, 'Get Lauren!'

'Yeah, get yer purdy liddle flower bird!' the love-witch echoed, thrusting her challengers into *my* face; so that, sucking down the last fumes of fire, I tossed my empty aside and, shivering a boozy chill, went to locate my sweet one.

There she was still, sitting next to Missie, smoking a j, gossiping. Stalking up, I grabbed her by a wrist and hoorayed 'Come on!' offering no explanation.

They looked at me startled. 'Hey!' she objected, trying to pull free. Some slogan sprayed out of my lips, and you know what? All of a sudden all intention to protest drained from her and, slipping a hand through my arm, she was upright beside me. A look of surprise morphed into one of anticipation. She straightened her skirt and let me lead her almost bodily to the bathroom, in whose door the three pioneer bathers stood nearly dressed while Curt and Vanity eyed the beige of their swill as it whipped around chipped enamel into a smeary plug-hole.

'Gonna take off some of that city slick?' the mountain guy wondered, helping himself to a stroke of my sweetie's hair. At this she shied like a filly, which maybe why he'd done it. Chortling good-timer-ly, he slid past us into the living-room.

Curt had begun barking with overdone emphasis, 'Yeah, we're gonna have us a bath!' And turning the taps on, he stripped himself naked and, slopping over the edge, lost his balance and,

pulling himself up, yodelled 'Liberate yourselves, motherfuckers!' spraying splash back at us.

Liberate yourselves… The time had come to pass through
another barrier: to have our ritual baptism into this far north-
ern-ness. I glanced at the women, Vanity leering like intoxica-
tion incarnate, Lauren eying me in modesty's pain. From behind
us came the buccaneer cry of brother Curt; and I had to make
a decision, for better or worse. So in the blink of an eye I was
naked too, teetering on the edge beside him and yelling like one
of Bacchus's satyrs for the gals to join in.

'Ain' nothin' to it. Jus' get naked an' leap!'

Our brains had switched off.

Vanity, glancing at Lauren, shook her blonde frizz. What did
it mean? that she knew? she could see? she could tell that my
sweetheart was made for affection, not daring? that she longed
for soul over strength, not lust or power? that beauty and its
understudy, sex-overtness, belonged to a realm alien to her? a
realm of stranger gods? phantom lordlings? creatures of some
dark overworld or abyss? Whatever Vanity knew or intuited –
and surely, it was much – she was soon bursting loose in a weird
huzzah of her own and, tearing her dress off, baring those ripe
cantaloupes. 'C'mon!' to my dearest she railed in Earth Mother
groan and, slipping her avoirdupois over the edge, slopped and
plopped into the drink next to us.

Lauren stared at me fearful, questioningly, tears set on the
rims of her eyes. So what did I do? Echoing 'Come on!' I glowered at her, tender and inviolate though she was. Grotesquely
I heaped incitement on aggression, braying 'Liberate yourself!'
out of spirit-burnt lips, watching as if from some smug height
above her with the other pagans. She wrestled whatever sow
of a demon had gripped her, and memory of it twists me still.
I'd committed myself, no matter what the act meant or didn't,
so now I was forcing her to choose between headlong descent
and a pristine innocence that was natively hers. The others were
yelling 'Come on!' browbeating her toward decision, hurrahing,
overbold. A slash of panic crossed her features, distorting them.

She forced out a laugh, then some weird imprecation and, dropping calico and lace to the floor, exposed that mildly proportioned, faintly freckled body...

We had done it. Innocence, seduced.

To Curt and Vanity, this was an excuse for more hooting. For me, it brought on an access of shame. I felt sobriety, yet at the same time exultation. She had done it! Lauren had chosen for *me*. She had humbled her*self* so that our conflicts could be solved. And wrapping her up there tight in my arms, I bathed her soft eyes in my reddened ones, trying to communicate what it was I felt: that I *knew*, understood that it wasn't for her to play bawdy games in a tub full of lascivious louts, even if in the name of some bogus *code*; some get-it-on, ersatz Dionysian orthodoxy.

The others continued their squealing and splashing, and rust-tinted water sloshed to the floor. Bravely we tried to join in their hilarity to cover the crudity of it. But new folks were passing the door now, gawking and sniggering or pointedly ignoring our urges to *get it on*! Mortification increasing, we belched it away with a rash pretence of daring. Otis chanced past and we had him almost convinced to come in, good solid Oaty, which might have justified the escapade in some way, or at least diluted the foolishness of it. But he went off to get Missie and, when *she* came and saw us, she screeched 'I can't! I just can't!' and while Oat tried to cajole her and Curt kept yodelling 'Liberate yourself, mo'fucks!', my poor darling could only shrivel into herself. Before long her new friend, disgusted, had turned heel, leaving Oat in the doorjamb trying to laugh it off, though by now he too was about as abashed as a tolerant ol' boy could be.

'Guess we showed this northern crowd!' Curt crowed, to which Vanity cawed, 'Showed the northern crowd?! Hey, they *need* some showin'!' And in one jigging mass she heaved all her glories up out of the tub, jugged them over the edge, sluicing waves out and back, and strode out into the living-room self-righteously crying, 'Come on, you fucking poof runts of a litter! Time to get *naked*, you boars 'n sows!'

Shutting her eyes, she spattered their faces with beads from her globes in a wild invitation to dance. The rest of us came more decorously up out of brine and wound towels around our shame to pat ourselves down. But then Curtis, bare as a frisking porker, broke free to chorus 'Come on!' in a grunt, 'or don't you have the balls to *really* party?'

At this, a group of crafties shook their judicious pates. Locks agitating, more than one rose to go. From his corner, the albino, glowing, impassive, eyed Curt and Vanity as if they were the scheduled floor-show. Reeling off in the direction of Hart, Vanity snagged him from the arms of the chair of the blonde. 'Come on, donkey dick!' she yowled, fantasy-drunk with a vision of the two of them leading us, leading the rest of the party or maybe leading the whole of a wildered north into some nirvana of orgy. 'Get your b-day suit on!' hooting, she crouched; 'let's see if *you* have the balls for it!' and, with dimpled ass shimming like jell-o, she set to unwinding the sash from his waist so as to yank down a pair of Mick Jagger-tight bell-bottoms. Thus the bare truth of our erstwhile Prince of Pirates could display itself in all its full gaudy of pride.

Hart froze. In stunned silence, as if carved out of wood, he smirked inanely. Wearing a grave scowl, Brother Michael made for the door. Vanity tugging, Hart remained still as a cigar-store Indian, until all of a sudden he must have caught a reflection of Curt romping in naked – a rival as if – because some infection of orgy seemed to take him and, no longer resistant, he lent her a hand to strip away the ruffed shirt and rest of a mufti she couldn't pull free. Pale, sallow, degenerate and defiantly insistent, he then was croaking 'Hey hey!' with a tongue thick from booze, 'let's get it on, people!' And taking her undulating flesh in two fists, he whirled her around, calling 'Come on, you fuckers!' hooting in glee while the glaze-eyed blondes simply stared china-cool, as if his drooped dick were no more than a hallucination to them, a fungus or matted dangle of grass rather than any totem to bow down to and worship.

Crafts people were crowding to exit as, spotting me by the bath, Hart spun around and, gripping my biceps, whipped me outward and forward into some version of devil- or ghost-dance. Not conscious, on instinct, I whirled him away. Recoiling, he spun like a top 'til he was banging the walls, revolving as if only to be brought to a stop by some piece of furniture crashed into or person prepared to help him recoup a last shred of his cast-to-the-four-winds dignity. Shameless Vanity continued her caricature of a waltz until, as if focusing on her for the first time, Hart froze anew. He could see now. He could see why the bodies were blocking his doorjamb to get away.

Brain flicking on, you could see him fill up with a galling, contrasting sort of energy. Groping back to his clothes, he struggled to pull on his pants. 'Don't go without me!' he called to the blonde and her shadow, floating in slipstream of a green and gold letterman's jacket. Then without another word to anyone else at his party, Hart followed those dim Lorelei into the night.

I walked past Oat and Missie to get my shirt, socks and boots.

'Guess you guys told that northern crowd,' he smirked.

The rest of the others sloped off while Lauren and I dressed. For a time then we sat there trying to rap to him and Missie. Laughing, we all strained for some prelapsarian joy, but eventually they had gotten up and were leaving too.

Like a boil that's been lanced, the poison drained away, leaving skin slack and empty. Vanity and Curt kept gliding around to hard rock that dripped down four bare walls like spent semen. Then they too had vanished, into deeper recesses, some remote den in that red-glowing house where somebody's sub-Sadean fantasy could spiral off into the dark.

We were alone then.

I switched off the record-player and gazed north out a window. All was bleakness, not a star or a moon or a hint of an ocean distant, hardly a sound; only black and more black or maybe a hint of coal grey in an overcast dome of the heavens.

Lauren had wound arms around me from behind. Resting her head against the nape of my neck, she held me there firm yet gentle in the lacy grid of her embrace.

5.

Acid glare came around an edge of the shade, waking me. Again, it was nauseatingly hot in that bag. Again, I had the visings of a hangover.

Thrashing around restless, I tried to find peace. Then her legs had entwined me, and a hand stroked my face.

'We leaving today?' she inquired.

My head pulsated. There was no hope – I was wretched. But some obscure joy in the pain lurked inside: some sense that I deserved everything I would get.

'You wanna?' I muttered.

'Don't you?'

I didn't answer. Finally, with effort, I pulled myself up.

'Sure,' I said, as if resolutely.

She enwrapped me again and, kissing my lips, held me down.

We stepped gingerly through the living-room, deserted now except for remains of the fray. I knocked at Hart's bedroom door; no answer. Hadn't he come back?

As we were turning to go, I heard a jingle of dog-tags and sniff-sniff at the jamb. Cracking the door, I let Curt's ex's pooch out. She jumped and licked at us, delighted to be free. In the fug behind her, wracked breaths kept a pace of deep sleep.

'Hart,' I rasped, 'you in there?'

One snarfle halted. 'Whaddaya want?' Curt's voice gruffed.

'Hey, man, where's Hart?'

'Gone to hell,' Vanity croaked from under a bulrush.

'Why?' Curtis asked.

'Cause we're gonna split. Think you can get yourself ready?'

They reverted to silence. You could hear her whispering.

'Y'all go without me,' is what he said. 'I'll hitch back.'

'You sure, man?'

'Sure I'm sure, man.' – Voice fading into pillow, or breast, 'Have a good trip.'

So we sealed their love-chamber.

Beyond the windows sky and ocean stayed as grey as if they'd been sucked by a vampire. There was an infinite melancholy in the flat view over roofs. This whole land of a so-called New Age seemed relentless and heavy and out of conviction opaque. Did the sun never shine on this edge of the world?

We passed through the tall grass out to our Beetle. Curt's ex's pooch followed and, when I closed the gate, rolled plaintive eyes up at us. 'No, girl,' Lauren said, stroking a soft muzzle, 'you have a new home now, for a few days...' As if understanding, it flopped in the path and, licking the scent of my love's touch off its nostrils, envied our godlike mobility.

We were getting into the car when a metallic green, low-riding Buick appeared on the horizon. Cruising uphill, its muffled engine growled. Humping the crest, it swerved toward us and stopped. Tinted windows obscured the pallor of the albino behind a leopard-skin-covered steering-wheel. Garlands of smoke wove a crown around the blonde beside him. Flanking her to the right behind wire-rimmed, violet lenses, you could just make out the jagged features of Hart.

'Far out, man; glad you here.' – I stepped over.

He rolled down a window. 'Know what happened?' he incanted in monotone, not looking at us. 'Rando... Got busted.'

'Fuck, man. What a drag.'

'Yeah... I guess someone he was dealing with tipped off those plainclothes dicks hanging out at the fair. Probably been pinning him all afternoon; popped him on his way t' the party.'

'What a drag!' Lauren joined me in chorusing.

'Yup... Ol' frizz-head's done it this time. I told him he'd been up to too much biz, not enough pleasure...'

I echoed the solemnity. 'Anything we can do, Hart?'

'We're heading for Oat and Missie's to scare up some bail, if those deadbeats're holding any cash. Pulled over when we saw you. What're you doing up so early?'

Hesitantly I explained, 'We were, like, goin' to blow, man.'

'Blow? You mean split? Hey, where to?'

'Homewards, I guess.'

He eyed us for a stretched-out second. Focusing on me – that is, as much as you could tell through the obscuring lenses – he let an ironic grin crinkle the edge of a lip. Holding that for a beat, he then swivelled his gaze back forward.

'Yeah, well... whatever, man. Guess we better be gettin' on up to Oat's. Too bad you folks couldn't stick around longer.'

'Thanks for everything, Hart.' I said, 'we had a great one...' But the garish machine was already sweeping away. And humping the next crest, it vanished, trailing an irreverent moan.

We got into the Beetle and made our way out of town. The pain of hangover clung onto me unwelcome, also a nauseating sense, a vague apprehension – of what? Almost of guilt.

In silence I brooded, toeing gas to the floor. Smiling Randolph, laughing Randy, clown of the pack, master of revels, carefree, full of vim... I didn't want to think about it. I didn't want to think about Hart either, though the brash features behind violet lenses stared out of the dim reaches of mind... It seemed as if he was fading, losing himself, dissolving back into a slough of native self-destructiveness. It was like he was willing the worst on himself, I mused, hardly noting an after-impression of envy, as if I had never secretly longed to take the same route but hadn't the daring to do so. – The daring! That's what made a legend, good or bad, huh? At the same time, it was what made a guy oddly helpless. So I pitied Hart then, as much or more so than Randy. And as I did, I realized he was dying in me again, this icon or hero of vanishing youth...

Pressing our Beetle down the highway, I tried to drive him and all of it out of my thrumming brain. We were headed south now, but those monster redwoods just kept marching in in formation, gathering as if to surround us, enwrap us, hold us in their weirdly compulsive, end-of-the-earth aura forever. They were so thick now suddenly, so uncompromisingly grand that you were almost eager to get free of them. But... Just north of Garberville, I recalled how I'd reacted against Hart and Co. in

39

this way before – a certain pique at his judgements, repulsion at the antics his code demanded – yet had always forgotten whatever it was, so that his influence had come back on me undiminished... Lauren beside me hummed in quietude, finishing those moccasins. Every now and then she'd look over and smile, mildly contented... On the other hand, I'd never felt Hart dying in me like this, during our halcyon days...

Gradually we veered inland. Overhanging clouds broke. We passed the shingled gas station and tavern where we'd stopped on our way north, then dropped down over the next county line. Here the redwoods stood out more sparsely amid pine and live oak on the progressively gentler hills.

Palo Alto, 1971

A COUNTRY HOUSE

I.

Two pairs of feet lit out along one of the paths the Duke of S_____ had carved through the beech groves of the old Stuart estate. May afternoon sun glinted between budding leaves. Racing, they came to a halt under the Great Oak next to which Prince Albert's friend, the American Lord A_____, had cut a view west down to the river.

'I won!' the blonder of the two proclaimed, throwing herself down on a bench.

'Only because your legs are longer,' the other gasped, collapsing beside her friend.

'I have to be faster. You're the more beautiful.'

'Right now I'm only the one more out of breath!'

The blonder of the girls closed her eyes and lay back.

'Helena?' the amber-haired one whispered, 'look!'

The girl called Helena opened her eyes to gaze round to where the other was pointing. 'The boat, you mean?'

'Yes! Let's fly down through the trees and leap on it!'

'And where will it take us?'

'O America, I think!'

'And why would we want to go there?'

'Freedom and riches and cowboys riding over the plains.'

Helena went pensive. 'You think it's like that?'

She rose and stepped over to an azalea just coming into bloom. Sunlight fell in shafts through the young beech leaves. She buried her head in the plant until her curls seemed almost to be a spray of daffodils thrusting up out of the pink.

'You remember your lines?' the other one asked, shaking a cascade of pre-Raphaelite glory: coral infused with gold.

'It's so lovely... How could you want to leave English spring-time for anywhere else?'

'I've never performed in a play before. Have you?'

Helena spread her arms as if to embrace the blossoms. 'Thousands upon thousands!' she mused.

'Have you done *A Midsummer Night's Dream*, then?'

Gathering a handful, she transported them back to the bench. 'It's your colour, Alivia, look! The pink is so gorgeous. Your hair is so beautiful – Hermia!'

'No, yours is!'

'No, yours is the more fine!'

'I thought mine was as "ugly as an Ethiope's"?'

'That's Lysander's line, silly.'

'I thought it was Demetrius'.'

Tossing the flowers into the air, Helena watched them fall in a shower over her would-be rival. 'You may think you don't know your lines now. I couldn't repeat a word of mine if you asked. But I'm not the slightest bit scared.'

'You're so much braver than I.'

'No, just sure it'll come right in the end. They'll tumble right out on the cue. And yours will too, or I'll pull them from you – just like those Ethiope hairs!'

The other girl, who was called Alivia, not Hermia as in the play, stretched herself over a patch of new grass.

'Will your parents be coming?' she wondered.

'My mother.'

'Not your father? – stepfather, I mean.'

'He'll be there too, I expect.'

'Mine as well.' – She went quiet.

'And your mum?'

'In America, isn't she?'

'With freedom and riches and great cowboys riding out over the plains?'

Alivia gazed down towards the river.

Lifting her eyes, Helena studied the leaves, which were sway-ing. High on a breeze, they made a susurrus, like a waterfall.

42

'What was he like?' Alivia asked. 'Your father, I mean.'

The sun winking down made her fail to respond. When finally she did, it was to ask, 'Do you mind being chased by Seb?'

Alivia was nonplussed. 'Not half as much as you mind chasing Angus.'

'I like them both better once they're transformed by Puck.'

'Then they're both chasing you!'

'On the other hand, I prefer chasing to being chaste, don't I?'

'You seem to like Angus chasing you well enough.'

'Angus Warburton can do as he pleases.'

'Did he last night?'

Helena turned to the azalea.

'It *was* Angus you were out with 'til the wee hours, wasn't it?'

'No. It was one of the groundskeepers. And we made raving love, down at the jetty. Then we stole a punt and set off for America. But we only got as far as Cookham Weir before a current caught us and he fell over and drowned.'

Alivia giggled. 'Did you really make love with Angus Warburton, then?'

Helena turned from the plant and stretched too in the grass.

'What was it like, Helena?... Helena?'

The sun hiding behind the pale green peered at her, then re-hid, then came out again in bared glory, then retreated again, or tried to, behind a translucence of leaves.

'You're not answering. Which must mean that you did; or you didn't. Or did you? Helena? Come on: you must say.'

'He was "handsome as the Pimpernel",' Helena murmured.

'Who? Angus Warburton?!'

'No, my father – real father... very blond and sunny and live-ly and dashing, and Mum adored him, absolutely. She's very silly sometimes, but he was extremely... I've seen pictures. Don't know what he saw in *her* of course, but she loved him to dis-traction and was devastated when it happened... That war has a great deal to answer for.'

Helena's father had been shot down in a Spitfire: every child in the school had heard the tale.

'How old were you then?' Alivia asked in a hush.

'I wasn't born yet. My mum was six months' pregnant. It was only days before the jerrys surrendered... Why? Don't you think it romantic?'

Alivia looked grave.

Suddenly Helena stood. 'Come on, then. Have to be in costume in an hour.'

'But... How old were you when she remarried?'

'I was my mother's husband until I was six,' Helena answered obscurely. 'And I did *not* make love to Angus bloody Warburton last night, or ever!' Pattering up to the path, she added, 'But I surely shall do so when I fancy!'

Alivia watched the yellow curls bob in and out of the blossoms. 'Maybe you will or maybe you won't... Or maybe I'll do it with Seb Buckingham first!'

'If you can catch him,' a plummy voice cried. 'And he isn't turned into an ass yet by Puck!'

'I thought you were utterly charming,' Mr Franklin effused in his Brookline, Massachusetts accent. 'And if it weren't for the fact that my stepdaughter was in the performance, I might've said you were the most utterly charming aspect of an utterly charming evening.'

Alivia simpered. Helena winced.

'Utterly charming,' Mrs Franklin chorused in clarinet lilt.

Helena looked away from her stepdad and mother, who was wearing a dun-brown twin-set. Impatiently she scanned the crowd milling around the 'Rule Britannia' amphitheatre where Sommerton School's production of *A Midsummer Night's Dream* had just ended.

'But Helena's much more accomplished than I,' Alivia intoned to her friend's parents. 'You can say so; I'm not bothered. She tells me she's done it a thousand times before.'

'"Done it"?' – Franklin turned to his stepchild. 'Helena dear, what have you "done" so often?'

Helena shot a look at Alivia. 'Dost thou mock, Ethiope?'

'Dost thou deserve to be mocked?'

The two dissolved into secretive giggles, under cover of which one led the other out of adult range. 'Must get away!'

'Where're you going? I want to come too.'

'Don't you have to see your dad?'

'But Helena, look!' – Alivia pointed to a break through the leaves where light faded in striations of salmon and gold.

'I know; we must hurry. But Alivia' – Helena pointed in the other direction to where an enormous orange ball rose heavy above the Chiltern hills – 'it's almost full. I saw it last night.'

'Are you going to the jetty again with Angus?'

'Angus or no Angus, I'm off!'

'Can't I come?'

'Of course, silly. Do as you please.'

'I'll bring Seb, shall I? Didn't you love him as Lysander?'

'If you want. Only let's get our duties done with and go!'

'Ssh, there's Angus... Can always pick him out – so tall.'

But Helena's attention had been deflected. 'Who's that man? No, not Angus – that one over there, by the burial urn.'

'O. That's my father.'

'*That*'s your father?'

Alivia beamed. She had something to impress her glamorous friend with at long last. 'I'll introduce you...'

Alec Featherstone had caught sight of his daughter just as she and her blonde friend had spotted him. Breaking off chat with Seb Buckingham, still in costume as Lysander, he eyed them in indulgence as they pattered up.

'Marvellous!' he exclaimed, catching each on an arm. 'Tell me, how does it feel to be such stars? This young man says if it were a midsummer night's dream truly, he'd have to have you both for not being able to choose!'

Sandy-haired Seb blushed pink as the sky.

Angus Warburton meanwhile, still in costume as Demetrius, sloped over. 'Going to the jetty?' he rasped to Helena.

'Ssssh!' she emitted, entranced by her friend's father, who was slim and fair and had hyacinth eyes. Despite his pinstripes, he seemed too young to be dad to a fifteen-year-old. Looks like my father must have, Helena imagined, and watched in envy as he continued to swing his child by an arm.

'It makes me nostalgic for *my* schooldays,' he was going on to Seb, 'though Sommerton's two-sex policy gives you lads an advantage over what we lot had at Eton.'

'Th' old poufter!' Angus murmured.

'Sssh!' Helena reprimanded; at which point the Franklins ambled into the group.

'A most charming, enlightened environment,' Helena's step-father purred. 'Not at all like the chilly, celibate ardours at my prep school in Groton. Lucky young people!'

'Very lucky young people,' Mrs Franklin echoed.

Alivia's dad took it up, 'Very lucky young people, indeed!' and bussed her on a cheek. Thereupon she introduced Helena's parents to him, and Helena introduced them to Angus and Seb, and small talk pit-patted round as the sky continued to fade. At last, before the Franklins had repeated themselves more than twice, Alivia's dad invited them down at The Ferry for a pint. The girls were inordinately grateful. As by the touch of an Oberon's wand, the older generation could vanish and they be free to plunge into the gloaming of Sommerton's woods.

Racing feet slapped down a lane to the river.

'I won!' Helena proclaimed, reaching the jetty.

'What do you want for a prize?' – Seb came in second.

'A kiss from Angus is what!' Alivia chimed, coming third.

Angus Warburton brought up the rear. 'What're we meant to be doing now?' he panted.

'We all disappear into the trees!'

'O let us rest first!'

'It's too dark for that,' Angus observed. 'What if one of you were to get lost?'

'*We*'re not going to get lost,' Helena chided. 'And if *you* do, you can always moan 'til the rest of us hear. Come on!' – She started down a bank towards the bronze orb rising.

'Wait for me!' Alivia cried.

'No, we go our separate ways. And once we've disappeared, each one tries to get back without the others finding him first.'

'That's too complicated,' Angus objected. 'What if – '

'Just give it a go, mate,' Seb cut him off.

'Shouldn't we at least limit the area?' called Alivia.

'Anywhere under the moooooooon!'

Helena darted into a thicket and was away. Racing to the east, she zigzagged up a hill, then turned again towards the river. A hundred metres on, she came into a grove of ashes and threw herself down. Rolling onto her back, she gazed at the intense silver reflecting off blackened leaves.

The ashes were luminous. The orb having shrunk was no longer orange; from gold to silver it was now turning white, and all around it light flickered, making magical shapes rise. An owl hooted. Listening to the strange cracklings of undergrowth and melody of the leaves and low murmur of the river in the distance, Helena forgot about her game, and Angus, and Alivia's question as to whether she were going to discover that big secret on some night like this and, if so, with what sort of bloke. The moon seemed to wink at her; it gave a broad, playful smile, like Alec Featherstone's. She was thinking again of someone vaguely like her father when from uphill she heard the owl hoot again and raised herself on an elbow to listen.

The sound repeated, but... was it an owl really? Another hoot... Could it have been Angus? Angus Warburton! Helena almost giggled as, imitating the sound, she lay flat again.

The hoot repeated itself, seeming to draw closer. Emitting a peep, she lay absolutely still.

A foot crunched on dry twiglets not far away, a man's step, and she thought – it *was* him!

The hoot sounded anew, very low, very near. She lay very still, until the feet were almost on top of her, then reached up and grabbed an ankle. A body came down –

'Helena!' Sebastian Buckingham exclaimed.

Glint of sandy hair. 'But... I thought you were Angus!'

'Well I'm not bloody Angus, thank you very much.'

He pulled himself up. She sat upright too.

'O Sebbie! I'm sorry, I thought – '

'Sssh! not so loud… They might find us.'

Something in his tone sounded other than bloke-ish Seb Buckingham of Sommerton School. It seemed older, more calculating than the normal, prank-playing lad's. Alivia's father again crossed her mind. An anonymous sprite had tripped into her moongrove, and she shivered in a rush of playful intimacy.

'Are you disappointed I'm not Alivia?'

'Are you that I'm not Angus?'

'Terribly!'

'I'm glad it's you, Helena.'

'"Those vows are Hermia's. Will you give o'er?"'

'"I had no judgement when to her I swore."'

'"Nor none in my mind, now that you give her o'er."'

'Don't I?'

Taking the chance as given, he leaned over and kissed her.

'"Lysander!"' she started. '"I fear thou dost mock!"'

'Not at all,' he murmured, drawing her close. 'I've loved you in secret this whole hour at least.'

The moon was high and sharp-focused by the time the four had recollected at the jetty. Angus had twisted his ankle on a root, so they made their way up to the house by a gentler path than the one they'd raced down. Seb led the way, Helena following, Alivia trailing her by a hand. Angus, who was too proud to accept their assistance, brought up the rear.

They went slowly on account of him. When the trees broke to reveal the sculpted lawns spreading up to the grand structure, they paused to allow him to rest.

'It looks like Versailles,' Alivia murmured.

'You think so?' Seb mused. 'I fancy it looks like a stately home designed by the architect who designed the Houses of Parliament, but missed out the Gothic bits.'

'It's a symbol of our heritage,' Angus spoke up. 'Bloody sad, too. All it is now is a place for a load of immature prats to rush about in the name of so-called free-expression under the complete licence of a so-called New Age school.'

'You're showing your colours, mate,' Sebastian scoffed. 'We can see what kind of reactionary you're going to turn into.'

Poor Angus's ankle pained him. 'I'm not going to turn into anything other than what I'm meant to be: an Englishman who believes in our great traditions, not all this daft freedom, running about like rabbits, breaking one's ankles and – '

'Your ankle's not broken,' Helena chided. 'And you ought to get it right about "tradition", even if you are a bit hurt. What were we playing at now if not *A Midsummer Night's Dream*?'

'O you're such a perfect Englishwoman,' Alivia murmured. 'You can rationalize anything, can't you, dear?'

II.

Angus Warburton's flat in Tite Street was decorated with Pre-Raphaelite *objet*s and Art Deco tat purchased in Portobello Road. Angus himself had donned the velveteen trousers, loose brocade shirts and bangles of the Carnaby Street set. Growing his hair long in the manner of Charles I, he wore a lash over one eye in a style later to be made famous by the hero of a cult film. His new bird, the sister of a current top model, was all flashing teeth and platinum coiffure.

Helena imagined her own bright curls somewhat tarnished by contrast. She felt out of place in 'swinging' London in her Newnham College blue-stocking gear. Seated on a pouf, she was abnormally quiet as Seb chatted abnormally loudly over 'Under My Thumb' by the Rolling Stones. What was Benedict Wesker thinking, she wondered, sipping Nescafé out of one of Angus's Byronic skull-mugs.

Helena had cajoled Seb into letting Benedict ride down from Cambridge with them. She had cajoled Benedict into coming to Angus's instead of going straight home to his parents in Hampstead Garden Suburb and was beginning to feel guilty about it. So it was as much to save Benedict as to please herself that she spoke up to suggest they go out for a day in the sun.

'O let's do!' toothy Crissy agreed.

'We can go to Portobello,' Angus offered.

'No, I mean out of London,' Helena clarified.

'But we've just arrived!' Seb protested.

'"Tire of London and you tire of Life,"' Angus declaimed.

'Tire of complaining of London, you mean.'

'Let's go to the country. It's too hot in town.'

'But where?' Crissy demanded. 'To your parents', Angy?'

'Can't. They're bloody there.'

'Why don't we go down to Sommerton?' Helena proposed, and Angus cast a sharp eye at the girl he had once lost to a rival in Sommerton School's woods.

This was not missed by Seb, who draped an arm over his bird's shoulders. 'Great idea, Helena m' dear. We'll all go down to Sommerton for the day. And bring that hashish with you, "Angy". I'm developing quite a taste for it.'

Sebastian placed Benedict with Crissy and Helena in the back of his cherry-red Jag and gave Angus the seat of honour in front, to 'look after sounds and the smoke'. The result was that, shortly, the fanfare and fog of Tite Street was permeating the young man's vehicular pride 'n joy.

'But you *can't* want to listen to classical music,' he objected. 'I thought you were all the new wave.'

'Yes, do put on Radio Luxembourg,' Crissy chimed in. 'They have a special on the Liverpool bands.'

Seb pushed a button on his Blaupunkt.

Angus pushed back to Radio 3. 'Good stuff, Beethoven.'

'Roll over Beethoven!' Seb said, repushing Radio Lux.

Angus repushed the 3rd programme. 'Just listen, you great Cambridge git: this is totally Dionysian!' And the *scherzo* of Beethoven's 9th sounded through a cloud of Afghani while he conducted an imaginary orchestra.

'Oxford! Thinks he's bloody Furtwängler,' Seb quipped.

'I want to listen to Radio Luxembourg!' whined Crissy.

Helena studied the King's Road bird who had succeeded her in Angus' affections. 'You mean you don't fancy your other half's "great tradition"?'

'O he can be such a bloody great public school twit!'

Angus continued to conduct the *scherzo* 'til it ended. 'Have it your way!' He grunted and re-pushed Radio Luxembourg.

Benedict turned from the window he'd been gazing out of. 'Why switch it now? The *adagio* is the one tender bit of the lot.'

This gave Seb cause to glance in his rearview.

'Yes, you have no taste!' Helena said, taking Benedict's part. 'It's the only movement in Beethoven with genuine serenity.'

'I think of it as like an English country summer day,' Benedict added, returning his gaze to the impressionist sky.

'It's perfectly lovely! Do switch it back, Seb.'

'O cahn't we have Gerry and the Pacemakers?' – Crissy.

Angus shook his cavalier locks. 'Women!'

'It's not bloody "women",' Helena snapped. 'Benedict agrees. Now will you switch it back, Sebastian bloody Buckingham?'

'And Bolshies,' Seb muttered to Angus. 'Have any more of that toke, me lad?'

The hashpipe passed. The cloud in the Jag thickened. Helena joined Benedict in gazing out at the day while Crissy sang along with 'How Do You Do What You Do to Me?'

'The radio is sufficient!' Angus suddenly bellowed, putting his dolly bird in a pout. 'You'll have Beethoven and bloody like it!' – He re-pressed to Radio 3.

The *adagio* was indeed lovely, Helena mused in the blessed quiet that followed. She had never listened to it properly, she realized, but now, as it carried on uninterrupted, she felt a great stillness coming around her, like the pastorale of the day. Seeing the strong, aquiline line of Benedict's profile gazing out, she felt more drawn to him and less to the others in her boyfriend's befogged Jaguar. Then, as quietly as it had begun, the *adagio* ended and first notes of the famous 4th movement began. 'O dear!... Back to the old *Stürm-und-Drang*.'

Benedict turned to her. 'Yes. Strange, isn't it? From such love-liness to this bourgeois, nationalist frenzy...'

Seb eyed the new man in his mirror. 'Don't *you* go all Bolshie on us now, mate; everyone knows this is the best bit.' And roar-ing his Jag into what had once been Sommerton School, he joined Angus chanting Schiller's 'Ode to Joy' in mock-German.

'Bloody Bolshies taken over,' the one said to the other as they approached the great house. 'Bloody National Trust, i'n' it?'

Helena stared in separate but equal shock at crowds troop-ing over their former domain. Crissy admired in oblivious rap-ture while Benedict eyed one of the Roman sarcophagi the first Duke of B_____ had imported to use as a rose-bed.

'Did you enjoy going to school here?' he asked Helena.

Distractedly, she evaded the question.

'O let's get into the woods as soon as we can!'

'Yeah,' Angus seconded, 'somewhere where a bloke can smoke his pipe in peace!'

'*Ja wohl!*' teutonicized Seb. 'Disgraceful the way they clump around smashing the grasses in their bloody hiking-shoes and screaming brats from Golders Green.'

They started down a lane to the Long Garden.

'What's wrong with you, then?' Angus demanded of Benedict, who walked with a limp.

It was either a defect of birth or the result of some childhood accident – Helena couldn't recall what a friend at Cambridge had told her. 'Leave it out, Angus!' she admonished. 'How would you like it if I asked why you had such a ruddy great sweat on your forehead all of the time?'

Angus sped up next to Crissy and Sebastian, leaving Helena to follow at Benedict's pace. Gradually, she began to breathe in the balmy air and gaze at the sunlight drifting down through cypress branches. 'Still into that bloody *adagio*,' she heard Angus mutter ahead; 'better watch it, me lad: I have it on best authority that the type goes fickle in these woods.'

'Let her go Bolshie if she wants to,' Seb shrugged. 'Race you to the amphitheatre?'

Helena had not known Sebastian Buckingham to race anywhere since they'd gone up to Cambridge. Did returning to
Sommerton inspire him, or was he just showing off? Glancing
around to Benedict as if he might know the answer, she saw that
he was eying her carefully.

'What do you see in the branches?' he asked.

'O, the sun winking at me is all.' – She blushed

When they got to the Long Garden, they discovered that a
troop of Australians had laid claim to the lawn for a picnic.

'Bloody tourists!' growled Angus. 'Don't they know this
place belongs to the students of Sommerton School?'

'On to the amphitheatre!' Sebastian hoorayed. 'We'll have
another blast at your peace-pipe there.'

'O cahn't we go in the house?' implored Crissy. 'I want to see
where you were in short trousers, Angy.'

'On to the amphitheatre!' Seb persisted.

'Yes, where a Prince of Wales first heard "Rule Britannia"
before all these bloody foreigner hottentots invaded.'

Seb dropped back to share a bit of Sommerton lore with the
limping guest. 'In 1751 Frederick Prince of Wales was killed by a
flying croquet ball on these very grounds.'

'On what grounds?' Angus crowed.

'On the grounds that he was the greatest ass ever to be Prince
of Wales!'

Angus guffawed. Crissy emitted a titter. Seb snatched Angus's
hashpipe.

Benedict was still eying Helena curiously as they passed a
cluster of rhododendron.

'We played *A Midsummer Night's Dream* here when I was a
girl,' she mused, emerging into the amphitheatre.

'That must have been lovely. Were you Titania?'

'No, I was...' Her voice was drowned by Angus and Seb
declaiming an old schoolboy improvisation:

Poor Fred'rick of Wales was the dull-witted son
Of England's dull-witted old king.
He spoke German instead of the mother tongue,
And shone on the croquet green,
Yes me lads,
And shone on the croquet green.

'The greatest ass yet to be England's heir,'
Is what old George the Second said.
Then a good squire dared — Poor Freddy, beware! —
To bowl a fast ball at his head,
Yes me lads,
To bowl a fast ball at his head.

Thereon hangs the tale of the dull-witted son
Of England's dull-witted old king.
His last words were German, not the mother tongue:
'Ich sterb on ze crotchet green!'
Yes me lads,
'Ich sterb on ze crotchet green!'

This drew not only titters from Crissy but a huzzah from a gaggle of holidaymakers from Hull who had made camp in an arbour nearby.

'Can't escape the mob.' Seb muttered, rolling an eye. 'Where can a bloke go to smoke in peace?'

'Let's carry on to the jetty,' Helena suggested.

'Bloody *Dumm Kopfs*!' raged Angus as the northerners joyfully cried out for more.

'Yes, let's go to the jetty,' Seb seconded. 'We can swim there.'

'But I didn't bring my bathing-costume!' – Crissy.

'Bloody *Dumm Kopfs*!' – Angus waved a fist and, with Sebastian rollicking alongside, led them down to the river, chanting the Ode to Joy in mock-German.

'He's going to row off with your woman if you don't do something,' Angus mocked.

'Come along, Seb: keep it up!' Helena called from the stern of the craft she and Benedict sat in, as if there were no truth in what Angus was saying.

Benedict strained to keep the 'Adagio' in front of the 'Britannia' so that Seb would not be able to make the flying leap needed to save or at least impress his vanishing girlfriend.

'Go get her, matey!' Angus continued inciting.

'O do keep it up, darling!' – Helena pretended to play along as Benedict rowed.

'How exciting!' trilled Crissy. 'Be careful!'

'I'll get her!' Seb cried, precariously balanced on Britannia's prow. 'I'll save incomparable Helen from that Trojan frog or whatever!' With which he leapt, or perhaps just fell and gave a flourish of leg to add style to his failure.

Angus guffawed. Crissy simpered. Benedict smiled subtly and kept rowing, while Helena leaned over the stern to watch her erstwhile boyfriend bob in green water, strands of weed in his hair. 'Are you all right, love?' – She tried not to laugh.

'Course I'm "all right", you bloody daft cow. Don't I look all right to you?'

Stung by his tone, she turned to Benedict and murmured, 'Shouldn't we slow down and pull him aboard?' But the Adagio was gliding away from Seb Buckingham as swiftly as the Britannia was speeding towards him. 'Go on, Helena, have your romance in the trees,' she could hear him call behind, 'we know what kind of woman you are!' and while scrambling to grab a gunwale, he pitched a protesting Angus and shrieking Crissy into the reedy, fast-flowing current. The three of them were struggling to hold the boat steady and climb in as the Adagio swirled onwards. By the time they had pulled themselves up and were stripping off drenched clothes, they were no more than dabs of pink disappearing beyond a bend on the horizon.

The Adagio continued, afternoon going silent around it. Helena listened to the lap of its oars but did not dare look at their rower. She was mortified by what Seb and Angus had said, though she knew it was true. She didn't want to admit it, but she *was* through with Seb now, and with Angus; through with the whole lot of them who were growing up into arrogant, supercilious twits, as Crissy might put it. Benedict Wesker was different, she imagined. He was the sole one of them who had any sensitivity, and she was glad she had cajoled him into coming out with her instead of going straight home to Hampstead Garden Suburb; and if she wanted to glide off with him, it was her right to do so, no matter what anyone said. Why after all should she allow herself to feel guilty because of these barbs from her lads of the past?

Turning back from the stern, she laid her head on a rail. Tactfully, Benedict said not a word, and the warm hum of day fell around them. Gazing up the steep banks to where the tall beeches stood proud, Helena watched their leaves twist back on a sough of the breeze, letting their fronts catch glints of sun, and she thought of how she loved the sight more than any other and how it reminded her of other days in her life or in the lives of others beyond what she had known. She wondered, for instance, if her mother had been rowed like this by her father: her real father with his dashing looks and romantic airs. Then she caught sight of a profusion of pink under the strands of a willow and she said, 'Can we go over there?'

The little craft stilled, revolved and slid under drooping tendrils of yellow and green. Helena stepped out and went over to an azalea. Burying her head in its blossoms, she transformed her curls into a bouquet of daffodils thrust out of emerald and mauve. 'It smells lovely!' she breathed.

Benedict drew the oars in and sat watching from the little craft. 'Your voice sounds like music,' he eventually offered.

Spreading her arms to embrace the flowers, Helena wondered about her old friend Alivia and how was she finding America, where she had gone. So absorbed was she in this that she almost didn't know what Benedict meant when he added,

'It's high but not strident, like some wind instrument... not so reedy as an oboe – clarinet maybe, played ever so soft...'

56

Hugging the blossoms, she could not look at him still, though his voice seemed quite like music too – baritone, other-worldly.

'I knew a girl once, in my school. It wasn't a school like this one, but a grammar school, in the East End. She was West Indian; I was infatuated with her. She had a voice like yours, like some exotic wind instrument, only deep, very deep. And she sang – professionally in the end. She would've loved this spot. She sang a song about a willow.'

Helena picked up the thread. 'Will you sing it for me?'

Benedict stared at the blossoms. 'I can't sing,' he confessed.

'O go on,' she chided.

So he recited half-chanting the Jamaican girl's song:

> I may not be your best —
> You know good ones
> Don't come by the score.
> If you've got something missing
> I'll help you look
> You can be sure.
> And if you want to be alone
> Or someone to share a laugh,
> Whatever you want me to
> All you gotta do is ask…
>
> I said I'm strong
>   Straight,
>   Willing
>   To be a
>   Shelter
>   In a storm
>   Your willow, oh willow,
> When the sun is out…

Helena had stretched herself over the bank, petals strewn beside her. The words came out happy, she thought, though with a melancholy to them. Was it nostalgia she was feeling as she gazed at the sun through the strands of the tree? She didn't listen so much as feel, and fell into a waking dream. So it was only some time after Benedict had finished that she said,

'So… What happened to her?'

'To who?'

'To the girl, who sang that song.'

He gazed at the water for such a long time that Helena began to wonder if she was dead.

'She sings in a pub now, in Islington. I'll take you to see her one day.'

Helena decided she could risk looking at him.

'And… Did you love her?'

He pondered. 'I've never been in love before. Have you?'

She gazed back at the filigreed sun and said nothing.

'Are you annoyed?' he asked after a further pause.

Entranced by the calmness, she said, 'Why? Should I be?'

'The others… Sebastian… Don't you want to get back?'

She shook her head *no*.

He was then a silhouette above her against wavy yellow-green. And it could have been almost any man, she imagined, who had stepped out of the low boat, lifting his lamed leg, and was lying down in the grass beside her.

Twilight was close by the time they made their way up the lane to the great house. A pheasant flared out of the brush in front of them, scurried away. Two steps on and Helena thought she heard an owl hoot. Finally, as they came up to where the trees parted and lawn spread up towards the balustrades, they stopped dead. The sun going down blazed in the tall windows of the house so that for a moment it seemed as if it were on fire. They stood transfixed. The moment passed only slowly. At last the sun set, a final flame flickered, and what was left seemed to smoulder like some dusky jewels under a copper-green sky, above which a single star shone.

'I'd give you a place like that if I was able,' he mused.

'But I wouldn't want a place like that,' she retorted. 'I went to school there once; that's all. Now I want something better.'

They continued up the sculpted gardens in silence. 'You'd be bored by a middle-class life in London, I should think.'

'Would I? But why would I want some old privilege like this? So unfair. As careless and corrupted as Angus and Seb.'

'*That?*' – Benedict marvelled at what a Duke of S_____ had built on foundations of the palace of the Dukes of B_____.

'Yes!' Helena declared. 'It might've been otherwise once, though I wouldn't bet on it. It might be something more in future, but not now. Best to leave it to the National Trust; at least that way it can't be any one person's plaything.'

'Who's being Bolshie now?' Benedict teased and, when she turned to challenge him – 'Aren't you afraid they'll trample over the gardens and spoil it?'

'Who, Angus and Sebbie?'

He chuckled. 'Think they've left without us?'

'Of course they have, darling. I never intended to go home with them in the first place. Did you?'

III.

Benny Wesker was five and had blond, curly hair and a sunny disposition that Helena believed was like her own. Jane Wesker was seven and had dark hair and a dreamy disposition that Helena put down to her ex. Jane doted on Benny and cared for him sweetly, except in odd perverse moments when she teased him to tears. Tony Thomas thought Helena's children a picture of Pre-Raphaelite grace. He was nearly as charmed by them as dismayed by the fact that their mother had not found a babysitter on this, their day-out to the country. Tony had something to say to the new woman in his life, but on the train as in many a recent hour in London he had found himself entertaining Jane and Benny instead with one of Wilde's fairy-tales.

'But why does the Young King have to give up his pretty things?' Benny inquired.

'Because he wants to be good!' Jane explained.

'I'm sorry; I do not understand,' complained Benny. 'Why does he have to give up his pretty things to be good?'

'Because there're other people in this world,' Tony found himself saying, 'and one can't always think only of pretty things and oneself. Where would you and your sister be, for instance, if your mother always did that?'

Benny Wesker knit his pale brows. His sister put an arm round his shoulders. The two of them stared inquisitively at this new man in their mum's life. As Tony continued his tale, they fell into a trance. Only once he had finished did they brighten and bounce off to other sights of the train.

'You were wonderful,' Helena said, cozying up to him.

'Did you like it?'

'They did, immensely.'

'I asked if you did,' her American boyfriend repeated. 'Don't you think Wilde's your most brilliant social philosopher since, say, Shakespeare?'

Helena smiled. 'You are amusing.'

'He had as fine a social conscience as Shaw, if not finer. And on top of that something far more valuable.'

'And what's that, my sweet?'

But the young man was in earnest. 'A sense of the supreme importance of giving into the temptation of being yourself!'

'And is that what you want?'

'Yes. And I want you to give into it too.'

'What do you mean, darling? Give into what?'

He was about to put words to a phrase he had been arranging in mind for some days when Benny and Jane reappeared.

'When're we going to get there, Mum?'

'Very soon, darlings.'

'Where is it we're going again? a castle?'

'No, it's your Mummy's old school.'

'I thought we were going to a castle,' Benny whined. 'I thought we were going to see knights and armour and swords!'

'Do pipe down! It used to be a castle for dukes and princes and great pompous people like that; then for a time it was mummy's school; then it was sold to the National Trust. Now it's been leased to an American University.'

Benny knit his brows. 'When it was a castle, did boys like the Young King live there?'

'Yes, beautiful young boys like you and –'

'What kind of people live there now?' little Jane asked. 'What is an American University?'

'It's a place like Tony's going to teach in one day. And the kind of people who live there are, I imagine, students very like what Tony was until recently.'

Helena winked at her lover. Her children ran back down the aisle in restored glee. 'I'm going to see the castle where the Young King lived!' Benny crowed. 'We're going to see Tony's friends!' little Jane added, not to be outdone.

Helena slipped a hand through Tony's arm. 'See? They're as charmed by you as I am.'

But the sky was as grey as the masonry of the house. And the roses in the Long Garden were only a memory amid bare, twisting branches. And the trees above the amphitheatre were skeletal black. And the children grew fractious as Helena led them through the grounds, and Tony withdrew, and she began to feel apprehensive. Near the Great Oak she paused for a moment; mercifully, Benny and Jane ran out ahead. Gazing down to the river where Alivia had once fancied a boat sailing west, she felt a wave of nostalgia akin to regret and turned to this sunny new man in her life who was eying her closely, so closely that without intending she found herself apologizing for the weather, the melancholy of the day, almost for England altogether.

Smiling back at her wanly, in a odd monotone he breathed:

> Under the greenwood tree
> Who loves to lie with me
> And turn his merry note
> Unto the sweet bird's throat
> Come hither, come hither, come hither.

> Here shall he see
> No enemy
> But winter and rough weather.

'O you're so wonderful!' – She threw her arms around his neck. 'Why is it that you, an American, can remind me so much of what England can be – what we *could* be – than an English man can nowadays?'

Tony Thomas gazed at the reflection of his eyes in her pale ones, of his hair in her blonde curls. Smothering her oxidizing breath with a kiss, he was about to proclaim how much he loved her when the children bounded back.

'I'm cold, Mummy!' Benny cried.

'I am too!' little Jane added through chattering teeth.

'I know, my lovelies; it's horrid, this winter. Come along. I'll show you inside this beautiful old country house…'

But the great hall was no longer as she remembered. Above the broad oaken staircase, Ramsey portraits of George II, Queen Caroline and Frederick, Prince of Wales, all in sumptuous robes and hose and garters, displayed none of the all-too-human qualities that had led a king to regard his son as an ass nor a prince to lose his mortal grandeur in the absurdity of a croquet match. This was annoying, and Helena complained to Tony that the portraits seemed 'unreal'. She was little more impressed by an outfit of chain-mail from the reign of Henry VIII that stood guard by a tapestry of St George spiking a dragon, which held Benny's attention for nearly two seconds. It was all coming to seem a failure, her long-planned day in the country. Jane clung to her side, asking questions in a tired monotone, and Tony drew off to read an inscription beneath a Sargent portrait of the Anglo-American Lord and Lady A_____, who had taken the place over in the era of Wilde.

Bundling the children off to explore on their own, Helena took a step towards him. No sooner had she done so than into the room burst a pair of teenaged American girls.

'O how cute!' the darker one exclaimed of Benny.

'And who are you?' the lighter one asked little Jane.

The pair beat a retreat to their mother. 'Who are they, Mum?'

'They must be students here, darling; it's all right.'

Jane clutched next to her brother in Helena's skirt.

'Mummy, when are we going to leave?'

'You don't want to leave yet, my darlings. We've just arrived.'

'But I'm hungry!' the child mewed.

'Me too!' the boy moaned.

'We were just going to lunch now,' one of the girls said. 'You could come with us to the students' dining-room…'

The other squatted to child eye-level.

Jane buried her head deeper into Mum's pleats.

'You're terribly kind,' Helena murmured. 'No darlings, Mummy will get you some lunch as soon as she's had a chance to show Tony a few things. Now don't squeak.'

'O why don't you let us take them to lunch?' the darker one surprised her by saying.

'Please!' echoed the other. 'We'll take fabulous care of them.'

'The other guys'll just love it.'

'They're so adorable!'

Benny and Jane peered at their admirers in growing curiosity. Helena looked to Tony, inquiringly.

He had turned from the portraits. 'They're hungry,' he shrugged. 'Why not let 'em? These girls'll take care of them fine. I wanted to say something to you on our own anyway…'

The image of her children wandering off with strangers filled Helena with inexpressible gloom. And this new man in her life was eying her closely now: too closely, she thought. Turning towards an enormous Tudor fireplace, she intuited that a critical moment for her was about to be reached, but she had no idea of how she was going to respond to it.

'I like it,' he began.

'You like what, my lovely?'

'The house, grounds, the feel… even if it is in winter.'

Smiling weakly, she waited.

'You look very old now,' he continued and, gazing through a tall window at the stony sky, she wondered how on earth he could be so cruel. 'I mean, in the best way,' he added.

'What way is that, then?'

'It's something special, Helena. I saw it the other night, too. It was late, and we were sitting on your sofa. You were tired and distant; I was talking – remember?'

'You often talk, darling. Remember what?'

'I've never known a woman who could, like, all of a sudden suggest – everything, every age, just sitting there quietly in one spot gazing off into nowhere. I looked at your profile like I'm looking at it now, and I thought to myself: this woman – I don't even know how old she is, and don't care! She may be forty, she may be sixty or eighty – whatever. There's something so wise about her, so alive. She's a middle-class Englishwoman with two kids in a cold house in a wintry city, but not just that. She's a proud, aging lady who's lived apart from her country for three decades in a 15th century villa with bougainvillaea spilling down over ochre tiled roofs and great cups of gold taking over sculptures in the courtyard... There was a play I saw last year in San Francisco and after I saw it I knew more than ever I had to come here to find you.'

'What play was that, then? One of your Wilde's?'

'Nothing so supercilious. It was Somerset Maugham; *The Circle*. I think Maugham is the most underrated playwright of that era – a much finer craftsman than Shaw, and without all the moralizing. The play was perfection. It was about an Englishwoman and her lover who'd run off to Italy when they were our age and left everything behind – her marriage and son, his brilliant political career...'

'And what happened to them, darling?'

'Life! Falling out of love and regret. Remorse, guilt, frivolity; more life; superficial, maddening inconsequence. And in the end, at the age of sixty or seventy, when she's a painted dame and he a crotchety old dispossessed squire, they come back to England. And you know what they find?'

'I expect you're going to tell me.'

'That life has gone on just as before. That her son has grown up and taken his place in society and married a girl who dreams of running off just like her. That men have pursued brilliant careers with all the pomp and chicanery he's given up. That in the end they're the happiest of all. So that, despite everything, they find they're in love again, just as much as when they first eloped. And so they go back to their tumble-down villa outside Florence, and frivolity and life, and live happily ever after.'

Helena shook her blonde curls. 'And this fairy-tale is what you're proposing for me?'

'Why not!' the American answered.

'You want me to abandon my life and come away with you?'

'Yes!' he repeated. 'Yes, that's exactly what I want you to do!'

Helena stared at this young man who was looking at her with all the radiance of Tuscan noon in his eyes. 'Let's go out on the balcony,' she said. 'I have something to say to you too…'

'I'll build you a house like this,' he interrupted. 'I'll make you the great stellar spirit to guide the ship of my dreams. Come with me tomorrow – today! – and live in San Francisco high on a hill with the skyscrapers gleaming in the sun out one window and light reflecting in their Italianate marble making them glow like crystal towers of the future. And out of another a Gothic cathedral like Notre Dame, and the sounds of the city below, and brown and green hills behind other cities in the distance across the Bay where the ships sail in and out under the Golden Gate. Come with me and I'll write stories like Scott Fitzgerald and you'll be my Zelda, only without the self-destruction and pain. I don't want to serve in some factory of a university lecturing on the beauties of Jacobean drama to kids who only want *Star Wars* or TV. I'll start a journal and bring the glories of your culture out to my new world. I'll buy a bookshop and build an empire and be Napoleon to your Josephine. We'll become the monarchs of all spiritual things. And one day when the carrion birds of envy are upon us, we'll fly away like great, wise old eagles to our aerie in Provence or wherever. I'll make you a palace, and you'll be my countess and I'll be your count. Young men can come and learn at your courts of *amor*. You'll be Eleanor of Aquitaine, the belle and romance of their world, and I won't be jealous. I won't lock you in cold towers. I'll love you and watch over and let you live out your genius in its full flower, because it is the truly great thing in this world!'

They were standing in a tile-roofed summer porch through whose Palladian arches the aging Duke of S_____ had watched many a long evening fade over the tops of wide cypresses spreading down the terraces below. 'I think it's the loveliest dream anyone's ever offered me,' Helena murmured. 'Only there's something so essential that you leave out.'

'Whatever you want, I'll get it for you.'

'In plain English, what about my children?'

A frown clouded the bright features. 'What about them?'

'Who's going to look after them?'

His brow drew in. 'What about their dad?'

'O your dreams, darling... Don't you understand how fragile they are? You're a man, not a god, even if you are an American inheriting the earth. Your dreams can so easily come down crash on your head and leave nothing but bitterness.'

'I don't follow you, Helena. Tell me straight: why can't he look after them, at least for a time? You've done your bit.'

She turned her profile to him.

'Isn't dead, is he?'

'Of course not,' she muttered.

'Then why should he be living it up all the time while you're tied down here?'

She shook her blonde curls. 'O you are so very, very... different from me.'

'No I'm not. We're like twins – you've said so yourself.'

She couldn't argue. It *was* what she had said, and ardently wished to be so, baseless though it was in fact. Laying her head against his chest, she conceded, 'Yes, in many ways you *are* the image of what I always wanted – so sunny and bright, romantic and high-flying; but…' She turned to the arches and, placing a hand against their cold stone, gazed over the trees to where a weak sun attempted to break through corpse grey.

'You still haven't told me why,' he said.

'Why what, my beauty?'

'Why your husband can't take them.'

'"It's impossible,"' she murmured after a pause, '"to live with someone who's wedded to an unrealisable, yet unkillable ideal"… That's what he used to say.'

'Fine, but what does it mean?'

'My father – real father, who I never saw – my dream of my father – stood between us. That's what Benedict said. Of course, it wasn't all – there were other things, more tawdry, mundane… England's simply not your sunny land of opportunity anymore in this phase of our history.'

'Exactly! Which is why someone from my phase has to make sure that this beautiful house and genius that is you doesn't go down the plughole.'

Helena laughed gently. 'You *are* so naïve.'

'Well naïveté isn't a sin! It may not even be a disability. What are all Shakespeare's comedies but vindications of it? Anyhow, you aren't answering my question. Why won't you come with me? Is it some dream of your father, like your husband said?'

'You may be more like my father than any man I know.'

'Then come with me! Make any fantasy out of me you want to! I'll be your father, if that's what you want. Only you have to choose me, tell me, guide me.'

'And my children?'

'How can we take them if we're going to be free?'

'Who *will* take them?'

'Helena, what makes you think they need you so much? They just went off with two girls who wanted nothing more than to look after them. They're beautiful kids – a prize to anybody.'

'Would you take them?'

'That's not the point. Children are independent beings, just like you. They have to become individuals; your mothering isn't necessarily going to make them what you want them to be. It may even do the opposite.'

'In any case, they're my responsibility.'

'They're *their* responsibility. They're the world's responsibility... We'll get money and put them in schools; your mother, or someone, can look after them.'

'My mother isn't right for them.'

'Helena – Helena, don't you see? They don't need your dream of perfect mothering like you think. Your responsibility isn't to them so much as to yourself – to make yourself grow into the completed possibilities of your genius. Come with me. Choose for Life! like Frieda Weekley with D. H. Lawrence.'

Helena laughed strangely. 'O I do love you!'

'And what does *that* mean?'

'But I'm not your Frieda, and you're not Lawrence, thank god; and you're asking the impossible, the absurd! That I should come away with you... O, you're a con-man like all your race in some ways. You can't seriously expect a woman to leave her children and go away with someone after two weeks, or even eight months, of however much bliss. Besides, what would you do – what would *I* do – while we were running to the other side of the world, chasing some impossible fantasy?'

'Don't you love me?' he asked.

'I adore you, but – '

'Then be brave, and trust me. Trust yourself. Trust Life. Trust what you really most deeply desire. As Wilde said, give in to that temptation!'

She ran a hand through her hair and gazed out from the arches as if to implore a dun sky. Hovering behind her, she felt his arms slip around and breath make a fog on the air.

'Think of the fond Italy of your imagination,' he added and, in that curious sing-song –

> Who doth ambition shun
> And loves to live in the sun
> Seeking for all she eats

And pleased with what she gets
Come hither, come hither, come hither.
Here shall she see
No enemy
But winter and rough weather.

Before he had finished, a cry of 'Mum!' broke the spell and
Benny and Jane were racing towards her. Behind them came
a swart, middle-aged dame in tweed suit and brown walking
shoes. 'Are you the mother of these children?' she demanded.

'I'm sorry. Have they been a nuisance?'

'They've been perfect angels. Nevertheless, it is quite a shock
to have children of this age appearing unattended in the students' dining-hall.'

'But the girls – '

'My dear woman, if you are going to bring them into the
world then you must be prepared to look after them. You can't
expect perfect strangers, however well-meaning, or our school,
to do it. What if one of them should fall down and break a leg?
I asked them where their mother was and they couldn't tell me!
And by the way, I must ask what you think you are doing here?
This is not a public place, you know. The National Trust does
not allow visitors in winter.'

'I went to school here,' Helena defended.

'I don't recall you among our students.'

'It was Sommerton School then. I was here as a girl.'

'Well that was some while ago, wasn't it? This is not
Sommerton School anymore and hasn't been for a decade
or more. This is the American Overseas University and in my
capacity as housekeeper I must inform you that unless you're on
some official purpose or a student or instructor has invited you,
in point of fact you are trespassing.'

IV.

She stepped on the throttle and swept past a green guard house where a liveried pensioner dozed. Speeding along the gravelled driveway, she noted in shock that the trees around the Long Garden had vanished; in their place a colony of semi-detached houses had sprung up. In the window of one a sign read Buckingham Development Ltd.. Parking her mother's old Rover as far from it as she could, she set out for the woods.

She was heartened to find that the amphitheatre still existed. Standing in its centre, she tried to recall lines she had recited in it a quarter of a century before. Vaguely she recalled how her russet-haired girlfriend and she had rivalled one another as Hermia and Helena in *A Midsummer Night's Dream*. Gazing up, she saw the sun glinting down through late March buds. It seemed to be winking at her.

She hurried along the path to the Great Oak, suppressing intimations of loss. A man approached from the other direction. 'Madame?' he called out in florid accent.

'Excuse me,' she murmured and, continuing flight, noticed that in spite of a dusky complexion he was wearing an English county gentleman's tweeds.

Throwing herself down on the bench by the Oak, she laid her head back. 'I'm old!' she thought in a spasm of anguish and for a moment shut her eyes. Opening them, she lit a Silk Cut and peered down through the aperture the Anglo-American Lord A_____ had cut through to a view of the river. To the west it was blocked: young boughs not yet pruned. A ribbon of water could be glimpsed flowing east; on it a pleasure boat moved.

She stood and confronted a profusion of pink. Crushing her half-smoked fag under foot, she turned and began up towards the house. Approaching the tiled summer porch where Tony Thomas had first asked her to go away with him, she noted that its pillars were now painted the same gaudy green as the guard house she'd passed on her way in. Why on earth, she pondered, would anyone want to put *paint* on those arches?

The sun blinked through translucence. She looked to where a mechanical susurrus was sounding over the buzz of midday. One gardener was mowing terraced lawns into thin arabesques; another was trimming hedgerows into crescents. Both were dark – Pakistani or some such, she assumed – and she veered instinctively back into the woods.

She would go to the river – yes. She would go to the jetty and perhaps take a boat, if boats here still existed. Then at the end of the garden she heard a cry and glanced back. From its glorious perch, the house seemed to be calling to her. Stately as ever, its front balcony was occupied by more dusky workmen, who seemed to be painting balustrades the same green as those Palladian arches. She stared. The cry came again, or a shout, and she saw a fine featured man coming down the lane towards her, the same one in an English country gent's tweeds. She turned again. A pheasant flapped out of the undergrowth and scurried away, half-flying above the ground. Helena followed until it vanished to the left. She herself ducked under an overhanging cypress to the right and issued out into riverside sun.

By the jetty she found another green guard house. Another pensioner in livery was sitting there, reading *The News of the World*. She turned again – it seemed as if she was always turning – and thought 'What am I doing here?' Starting back towards the house, she heard 'Madame!' again in unidentifiable accent and, peering through another cypress, saw in shadows and glints the man in tweed bearing down on her. 'Who *are* these people?!' she protested under her breath and dove into the brush and trotted along the bank for a hundred yards before, panting and wheezy, she came to a clearing where a broad willow stood. For a time she gazed back but detected no one. Satisfied that she was alone now at last, she sat down in the grass, unlaced her mother's old walking-shoes and set to massaging her feet.

Melancholy came on the heels of adrenalin fall. Stretching her legs, she lay back and re-closed her eyes. Insistently the sun made patterns on her lids; the long yellow strands of the tree seemed to sigh in response to a faint moan in the breeze. She glimpsed a ghost of her dear Benedict; then everything was dissolving into more and more formless reverie…

'Helena!' a voice cried.

She lifted her head.

'Helena? Helena, can it be *you*?'

An amber-haired woman was rowing a boat towards her. Blinking, she sat up, grasping her knees. It took a long moment more before she recognized her old friend Alivia Featherstone bobbing over an undulation of water up to her.

'Helena darling – what a *surprise*! But… how in the world… You didn't come – you didn't just traipse all through Hassan's sacred wood, did you? He keeps all the entrances guarded, what with security threats and so on.'

'Alivia! Yes – who *are* these people? Someone followed me nearly all the way to the river. Finally I just had to flee through the nettles like some frightened bird. What on earth has become of our dear Sommerton School?'

'O it's still here, after a fashion. But Helena! – I've thought of you so! I've intended to get in touch, but… O life's been very full! Only you must tell me about yours, now that this miracle of you wandering over his enchanted land has brought you to me. What's been happening? You've hardly changed.'

Helena put a hand to her freshly-done curls. 'I must've aged terribly. But look at you! You look *exactly* the same.'

Her old chum chuckled. 'You always did irony.'

There was a touch of America in this, as in the jeans and checked blouse which Alivia wore with sleeves rolled up to the elbow. She continued to smile, a gentle mischief turning up the corners of her mouth as her eyes travelled to the brown shoes side by side at Helena's feet.

'I wasn't expecting to see anyone I knew, certainly no one so chic. These old rags – not what I wear normally. Mum's. She died last week. I've just been in Oxford to help my stepdad and stopped by here on my way back to town.'

'O Helena! I *am* sorry.'

'Mum was quite a silly bird in her way – don't let's be morbid. Her life was all that middle-class, county thing; I'm more interested in yours, Livvy. What are you doing here? How have you been filling the years since we knew one another?'

'Ah well… It's been difficult sometimes, and wonderful others – just like yours, I should think, and you *must* tell me all. Come into this boat and we'll row out in the sun, not under this tree – makes me sad. Doesn't it you?'

So Helena climbed into the prow of the little craft, and Alivia plied the oars or mostly just let them drift as she told about numberless things. She told about how she had gone to college in California but dropped out and lived in a commune in San Francisco and delighted in the crazy American freedom but eventually grew bored and longed to be back in England, whereupon she returned to divide her time between Chelsea and her father's place in country. She described how an American lad had followed her and how they had loved one another and broken up and got back together in Europe and California and various places in between, or beyond, and how she had gone to live in the redwoods with him and helped him build a boat in which they intended to sail across the Pacific but how that dream had faded and finally run into the ground. To all this Helena listened in gathering silence, resting her head on a gunwale and gazing in gradual dreaminess at the sun flitting in between soughing jade and lime-green. She recalled the choice she had made when Tony Thomas had offered her a life like the one Alivia was describing and began to hate her decision and all the years that had followed. Indeed, by the time her old friend had finished her saga, Helena had begun to so hate her own life of quiet desperation, as she now saw it, that a perverse will laid its hand upon her. So when her turn came to relate *her* adventures, at first tentatively and then with growing assurance she said:

'I married a Jewish man when I was at Cambridge; we were terribly in love for a time and moved down to London, and before I knew what had happened I was the mother of two beautiful children, a girl and two years later a boy. Benedict was a journalist, at least at the start; then something happened, and things grew awkward. We had little money and I found it hard to bring up the children with him struggling so, so I took a job teaching and it was all right; only his career was going from bad to worse – maybe I had something to do with it as he accused – anyhow, we kept growing apart, until suddenly things snapped and... O Livvy, it's so difficult for men in England nowadays – things happened that weren't at all what we had dreamt of, and it was awful for the children... until finally something so dreadful happened that we had to split apart.'

'O Helena!' her friend murmured, and waited.

'I took the kids on my own, and it was a struggle. But I kept teaching and made ends meet somehow. I thought that life was behind me – that all the adventure and wonder had passed. But then I met an American boy, just like you, and he loved me – O! He was a con-man too in some ways, but he persuaded me that if I didn't "choose for Life", as he put it, I might never have the chance again – that I'd grow into a tedious, old middle-class bag like my mother, only worse the way things have come down nowadays. So I did.'

'You "did"? You did what, Helena?'

'I took life by the throat. I did the most appalling thing a woman can do, Livvy... Sometimes now I think I would never have done it were it not for that unspeakable woman who challenged me at a critical moment with all our received opinion about mothering, but... I gave up my children. I gave up my country and went away with him.'

'You gave up your *children*?!'

Helena felt reckless. 'Yes! And why not? Children are individuals too, you know; they have their own ways to make in this world, like everyone else, so why should I have been tied to them anymore than you were to your country where there's no opportunity left except for the back-sliding Seb Buckinghams?'

'But Helena! it sounds so... I mean, don't you feel – '

'Why should I feel, or have felt, anything except joy at going off with a man who loved me and offered me the freedom to be my*self*? free of all the chains of the past – children, country, our self-righteous middle-class cant... No, I refuse to feel guilty! There were others to care for them, others with responsibility. Benedict had finished his cure and got a job at *Time Out*, and my mother wasn't doing anything of importance except terminally deferring to my stepfather... I left my beautiful children with them, yes! I went off with the sunny lad who loved me and who I'd always wanted in my deepest dreams!'

The afternoon had gone quiet, as if holding its breath.

'And so...' Alivia asked half in a hush, straining not to be judgemental. 'What happened then?'

'We were beautiful twins, Livvy! We were bright birds of passage! We were Frieda and Lawrence, and like them we took to the world! First we lived in San Francisco high on a hill, with the city spread out beneath us in the golden California light; and he wrote sonnets for me, and we put them to music, and no one was listening, but we didn't care, we were so in love – so truly, madly, deeply in love with one another and every great thing! But... Whatever happens to dreams, darling? We were going to Italy, except it was another place we ended, distant, more primitive. We ran off from the world – California, all of it. We put that behind us and discovered strange, wilder places – the south; a brilliant, killing sun. Mexico we went to and lived down on the coast, at the edge of the jungle. We had a fisherman's shack with a roof of palm fronds, and it was so simple, so spare. We lived off the fruit of the trees and lounged in the warmth of the day and made love in the nights. We had a little boat – not much bigger than this one. We called it the *Allegro* and went about sailing turquoise seas, out and out further towards coral sunsets. And then came that storm... We were swept away in a tempest – it was terrible! horrible! I can tell you... We fought for our little boat – our sail ripped to shreds – until, finally, in one of those great, unearthly cold waves it capsized... I clung to the boards and screamed out and screamed out, but... It was finished. He had vanished. Swallowed up by that merciless, indifferent, ugly grey-green of the sea...'

'My life feels so small,' Alivia murmured.

'All lives are small,' Helena echoed sepulchrally, her eyes wide and wild, though she felt oddly calmed. A strange will lifting from her seemed to fly off through the leaves.

'Helena?' a voice said as the faery or ghost passed, and a gust of breeze let her look at the sun again without cloud.

'Good-bye, father,' she murmured.

'Helena ?' – Silence.

'Aren't these grounds fantastic?' she shifted brightly to say.

'Yes, and I'm so happy to be here again, but... Helena, I always imagined you still in England, among the flowers, while I was over there. That was part of the reason I had to come back.'

Helena eyed her old friend now with cool indulgence. 'Perhaps some idea of you over there was part of the reason I had to imagine going away.'

'... Imagine?'

The word floated. 'O, I never ran off with Anthony Thomas,' she answered. 'Nor would I *ever* abandon my children. I've been here the whole time!'

'O Helena, you... little... prevaricator!'

'Well I am sorry. I have no idea what possessed me. I wanted to go with him, of course; and he did ask me, more than once. But... you don't mind so awfully me making it up, do you? We who stay home must have our fantasies too. It's nothing much worse than a spring afternoon's dream.'

Alivia studied her friend with unusual earnestness, as if trying to fathom deceit in a soul she had once thought she knew almost as well as her own. Relief came in stutters, her features held rigid until Helena's apparent ease made them start to relax. Annoyance passing, the two were at last bobbing on top of the waters merry again, as if a pair of teenagers out for nothing more than a gossip under the leaves.

'Isn't life strange?' the amber-haired one said. 'Do you know that Angus Warburton, with all his pomp, is running a bistro for the English crowd in L.A.?'

'And is that toothy King's Road bird still with him?'

'Crissy? Isn't she the limit? But just the thing for our "Angy", I should think. Saw them last time we were out there.'

'And we know about Seb Buckingham,' Helena mused.

'Disgraceful, isn't it? I can hardly forgive myself for having introduced him to Hassan. Now he thinks he's going to be the richest developer in Berkshire, cozying up to oil lucre.'

'Is that what bought the place?'

'Yes, and is painting it that revolting "Saudi" green. But Hassan's quite sweet really – must tell you... We've had our troubles too. Dad, you remember?'

'Your father?'

'Yes, well: seeing the demise of England, he wanted to make too much too quickly, to keep the house in the country and one for me up in town. I told him not to worry: I have my Mum in Manhattan, who's nicely fixed; but he was insistent that I have a life over here too; so to cut a long story short, he got mixed up in that dreadful banking scandal in the Gulf – you must've read about it, though he managed to keep much of it hushed. But he was ruined – finished among the people who knew. So we lost the place in Chelsea and had to give up Marlow too.'

'O Livvy! That sounds more like the true fate of our island these days... I thought your dad a really lovely person the one time I met him. Where is he now?'

'Well, if I can get these oars moving...'

'You mean – you don't *live* here?'

'My bloke – Dad could never handle us getting married – had some dealings with some Arabs some time ago and, through an American contact, met an emir interested in a place like this one. So that's how we got to know Hassan. Daddy helped to grease a palm, and the poor dear – Hassan, that is – well... in spite of all the green paint, he does long for taste really. He's taken to Daddy like a young Greek to Socrates, even to wearing a English country gent's mufti!'

'Ah. Spotted him, I think.'

'You must have. All over the place. Bit too much really – have to give him tea every day. He lets us that little rose cottage just up the path west of the jetty.'

'The "rose cottage"?'

'Yup. Where Angus Warburton stumbled on me that time we played your vanishing game after *A Midsummer Night's Dream.*'

'Alivia! You don't mean to tell me that you and Angus – '

'Well what do you expect after I saw Seb running off after you? And then poor Angus twisting his ankle like that... Somebody had to console him.'

Helena eyed her old chum. Alivia tried to suppress a titter, but failed. And shortly the two of them were giggling like young teens again in their tipsy conveyance.

'Intriguer!'

'I guess we're old enough now to confess our peccadilloes, aren't we? – But look, will you? That's what our grand olde English dream has come down to...'

Through a grove to the west, Helena spied two figures idling on a patch of manicured lawn. One was a dark, finely-etched, youngish man in wellies, the other light-haired older one in coveralls, holding a pair of secateurs.

'Hassan simply cannot understand how "a fine English gentleman", as he calls Dad, could be content to spend his days tending a rose bush.'

'They really are the limit, these Orientals, aren't they?'

'When he arrived in his caftans and what-not, the place was simply a parade day and night of "girls" down from town. My eyes were on stilts. But Daddy said to be cool, and you know what? The poor bloke isn't truly one of those ghastly whoremongers one hears about but a fascinated little boy wanting to know all he can about "Western culture", as he puts it. Now I have the greatest difficulty in not laughing in his face sometimes – he simply insists he must marry "a respectable, well-born English woman" and keeps at me to produce one for him!'

'Fancies you, I should think.'

'But I'm taken, darling. Come to think of it, what about you? Wouldn't you be tempted by his vast riches to be *châtelaine* of this gorgeous place?'

Helena lingered over the prospect. 'It's kind of you to offer. But how could you be content being my vassal?'

'O I don't think I should mind terribly. I could always run off to America if you got *too* bossy.'

Helena gazed for a spell at the sun through the leaves. At length she answered, 'Having resisted temptation once, I may find it easier a second time. Besides, at least one part of what I told you is precisely the truth.'

'Which part is that, then?'

'I do have the two most beautiful children up in London.'

Alivia winced. 'I wanted to have kids myself once. Left it a bit late, I expect. Anyway, I've never been quite the perfect Englishwoman you are, Helena. I've spent half my life chasing an American boy who simply insists that he loves me!'

San Francisco, 1978

THE HIEROPHANT

10.

KINGDOM of light is what we stepped into on that mid-morning, late. The sky above the Zattere was without mist, though a heat-haze was coming. Far ahead a young man and his mentor, still in student incarnation, were sitting in wait on one of the wooden platforms that extend into Canale alla Giudecca. The water was its familiar oily green. The brick edifice of Molino Stucky on the far side was not yet renovated into the package-tour palace it would become decades on. Cruise ships as high as tenements of the Ghetto did not obstruct our view; gondolas were still vulgar conveyances, vaporetti one price for all. It was the late 1960s. Harry's Bar recalled Hemingway; an English director had only just made *Don't Look Now*; and I was still murmured about when crossing the Accademia Bridge to listen to Monteverdi at La Fenice.

The platform on which the pair sprawled – I use the term accurately – was opposite a café in which we (I had my beloved still then) took lunch on days as fine as this one. We would sit on the pavement eying a horizon of palazzi diminishing towards the Redentore. It is a famous sight, justly. One does not tire of it. The restaurant too – I said café: it was both – tired us neither. They knew we would come then – on such days we were like clockwork – and find one of the tables the sole waiter was at that moment assembling. We were fond of that waiter. He would reserve just the right spot for us given season and angle of light until thirty minutes past our accustomed hour. Exact in all matters, he wore dark trousers, a white jacket immaculate, leather shoes polished and hair cut and oiled as if in a Fascist or an early American talkie film. It would be invidious to say that

he brought back a tramp-tramp of boots and cries of *Duce! Duce!*
On the other hand, he favoured black shirts and white bow-ties
instead of the reverse, and his expression towards the youths dis-
porting themselves on the platform was impassive at best. An
underlook of contempt could be detected. Nor from his point
of view was this inapt.

I recall Eugenio Pacelli – Pius XII to you – and a lifelong aver-
sion he tried to fight down – unsuccessfully, it seems – for fecund
Marxist women. Armpits unshaven and Fellini-esque bosoms
loose beneath flimsy frocks, a covey of them had attacked his
limousine when Papal legate during the Eisner rising at Munich.
The heat and odour, irreverence and no doubt prick-baiting of
these apparent harpies must have frightened that precious soul
as much as the submachine guns toted by their escort. Echoes
of those times reverberated in this decade, whose style adver-
tised itself as *against*: against war, against racism, against sexual
continence, against drug laws and all rules of an *ancien régime*
such as persisted. The two on the platform above the green
water were dressed in the patched jeans which were the uniform of their kind. Their hair was so long and unruly that, if it
hadn't been for a down of pale moustache on one and Rasputin-
like hang of goatee on the other, you might have taken them
to be Sapphists. My darling was amused when they appeared
to embrace; meanwhile the waiter, whom I eyed from our distance, seemed to recoil. 'Delightful,' she purred, and you could
feel cougar instincts stir in her still lovely limbs. Whether they
were what we would soon be calling 'gay' hardly concerned her:
perhaps they themselves didn't know. They knew little then, at
least the one who had come to find me. The other? He'd been
dragged along merely as *de rigueur* 'sidekick'.

Let me tell you what I saw from a score of metres away. We
were passing the Gesuati and had not yet been spotted when the
one in goatee, catching the glare in the eye of the waiter, and the
moustachioed other, seeing his friend pause, curtailed cheer-
ful banter to look around. The scowl of the native, fierce for
a flash as an eagle's, did not register on an inexperienced mind

sufficiently to discourage a blithe spirit from thinking to toss out some We-Are-All-One-ish line such as 'Hey man, you wanna…' presumably 'toke' on what he had been inhaling. But Rasputin, seeing a carabiniere in front of the port office a few steps on, put a hand on the nape of his compatriot's neck to restrain him. This one was cautious: I'll give him that – the alertness of the sly. The other went quiet; meanwhile, the waiter, watching the hand slide from nape to shoulder and then triceps to squeeze, flicked his rag at a pestiferous bug and returned to setting out chairs. At this, the one with faint down of moustache shrugged and, grinning again – a look which made my beloved purr – sucked on the cigarette he'd been fixing to pass to a 'fascist' before handing it, rank with Universal Love, to Rasputin. The latter, having loosened his admonitory grip, settled into something resembling lotus-posture to commence intoning 'Om'.

It is important to make clear what I mean by detailing this picture. People claim I'm obscure, but in fact I remain as I have always been, the simplest principle on earth. Unimpressed by downy saints, I rated our Rasputin higher, though not by so much as to want to take him either. I could see that they already had more potential (smoke-rings in fusillade towards the restaurant showed) than an American couple crossing our path, dressed Nixonianly in synthetic fabrics too loud and too loose – though, as my beloved observed, who would have wanted to see the lines of *those* forms via haunch-hugging shorts or knitted jerseys? The man padded forward on *faux*-leather loafers, the woman in walking-shoes of a style bringing to mind fat-footed hippos doing 'The Dance of the Hours' in *Fantasia*. Her hair bee-hived and faintly frosted pink trembled in *froideur* as she entered the aromatic nimbus around the boys and, when her husband grinned, she yanked him summarily towards a menu the waiter had just set out on a stand beside his clean, well-lighted place. A moment's harmony between satiric looks on the boys, eying the rumps of what might have been their parents, and scowl of the waiter who, flicking his towel, offered no welcome to these potential clients, masters of the world since Europe's fall in the

'40s and reducers of such chic as his pride sought to maintain. The moustachioed one, encouraged by this flash of sympathy in a 'wop', despite attributes which back home would have branded him a 'pig', overegged a desire to mark himself off from his 'ugly' compatriots by pulling a face behind their backs and, going over-the-top, making with bent forearms and bowed thighs as if to fornicate the female. Rasputin chuckled from within Buddha squat while my darling purred the endearing 'Ah!' of one ever ready to educate the naïve. The waiter, wishing solidarity with riff-raff no more than with its styleless elders, muttered a curse almost audible at my remove and, lashing his rag at another impertinent bug, vanished into the bar to wind down its awning. It was at this moment, protégé still playing the fool, that the Satanic *Om*-er turned our direction and, catching sight of what he would later describe in that tiresome memoir as an agèd, frail man in black sombrero and green Sherlock Holmes cape supported on one side by an ebony walking-stick and on the other by a bohemianly clad dame ('I was wearing Chanel!' my dear would protest) clearly younger than he, though well beyond sixty ('I was not and never have been a day over 45!'), relaxed his lotus posture and, again grasping his pal, hand around ankle this time, intoned 'ssshh!' (we had drawn close enough to hear), making the moustached one, still pulling a face for the waiter, who had resumed his station at the edge of his space from where, spying us, he stood to attention, respond 'Wha'?' To this the first, cocking his head, murmured 'There!', to which the other burst 'Where? What, man?' to which the wiser of the pair whispered, 'Pull yourself together, bro'. And remember: we represent everything he hates.'

It was of course untrue. I hated nothing. Hatred is a waste of spirit and no attitude one in my position should be capable of. Disappointment, disquiet, disdain – these are conditions of response I know better than most; but a passion like hatred? Only the uninitiated could ascribe it to an entity like me. But he didn't realize that, not yet, cleverer than his confrère though he may have been; and the fact that he didn't and, without consciously admitting it to himself, intuited it, is one reason he had positioned them there to chart my progress. Mystery, a sense of deep knowledge and experience beyond... that I should have evoked these for them in that era of gurus neither surprised me nor activated my *amour-propre*. It was not a status I sought – whyever would I? – merely one I accepted with such grace as was needful and no falsely humble demur.

We proceeded, my beloved and I, stately, debonair ('with feeble step,' he would write!) Downy moustache, having turned pretty eyes on us – 'like opals,' she murmured – grew sober, intent. Music had begun to float on air: the waiter, it seems, had switched on his victrola (Vivaldi, *andantino*) in deference to our approach. As we reached the periphery of his domain, he discarded all recall of *Il Duce*'s grimace to take on the smile of *Il Cortegiano*. Spreading an arm out, he turned his back on the boys and ushered us in to the spot he assumed we would favour. As we inched forward, I caught from the corner of a hawk's eye the dark one discarding his bodhisattva pose and, phantoms of Siddhartha flitting away, rise in hopes of attracting our attention. Of course I paid him no heed, though my partner could not resist glancing over a shoulder at Moustache, whom his mentor continued to clutch in restraint. A matador-like swivel on the part of the waiter obscured them: he pulled a table half under the awning and half out so I could shuffle into the dark space behind and she remain in the bright. With back to café I completed this move, squinting up as if to assess the range and trajectory of light, then dropping onto my seat with the exaggerated *hrmph* of one grateful to be allowed off his pins. My darling fussed while the waiter re-adjusted the awning so that whatever I had been shading with an upraised hand could be blotted out fully. Wasn't even the marvellous pearl-blue of Venice too much for a creased visage that, in their view, had seen All? Such was the message of our *pas de trois*, that and pretence that my condition was too grave for us to note that we were still being inspected and chance for an approach being sought. Ceremony, severe and forbidding. My beloved, having calculated the effect of a smile, countered it with the fact of a frown and, as if indifferent or no longer aware, engaged the waiter in a mellow Italian, partly veiling her origins as well as his native patois, on the topic of how one might cater in *Essen und Trinken* for the old master's needs on this fine *mezzogiorno*, given vicissitudes of spirit since we had last alighted at his fair *établissement*.

9.

FOUNDATION for those young men might have been a sense of sure values. I'm afraid they had not grasped any yet. They hadn't thought enough, hadn't lived enough, hadn't read sufficiently. They had heard music, but not of the spheres. They had observed art, but little more than cartoons. Philosophy and religion had gone no further than pop-song lyrics for them. In sum, apart from what they had gleaned in school, much of it by rote, they had their education before them.

Beyond you could see, if you skryed, clapboard houses, northern woods, gold and silver light filtering through canopy evergreens. They were forest creatures, not much better or worse than the dogs or the ponies they would fondly have kept had they not been the spawn of suburban *mores*. They wore beads and caftans, as if desert Arabs or shtetl Jews. American Indians were an ideal for them, as were Eastern ascetics. Their pose was about essence less than theatre *vs* what they had come from – the air-conditioned nightmare, etc. - in favour of an *other* as it appeared to them: fructifying chaos, anti-material, so said; a 'new age', as some called it – an order of make-believe, in fact. This had certain promise and temporal fascination, especially if you were young and could gather by some charm or other – luck in a parent, an open hand in a pocket – the wherewithal simply to *be*. Otherwise... But 'let's not go there', as they might say; because for them *otherwise*, though vivid beyond their suburbs, was 'real' as yet only in theory.

They lingered three days to get satisfaction from me. I spoke in cryptic monosyllable. They were unprepared; one could hardly waste one's breath. But they babbled on – that is, *he* did: Rasputin. The other let himself be eyed by my darling, who offered him titbits to feed a glazed stare. What did she see there? Not what I did. Emptiness appealed to her: the *tabula rasa*. For me it stretched out into vistas of wayward youth on pilgrimage to nowhere they knew of, searching for redemption in whatever face they might meet. Behind them straggled a motley troupe, angelic to some, merely wearisome to others, if not worse: prospectively demonic. Envisage the lanky and crimped, the dark and the fair, the sharp-featured and dull, the young women seeking, the young men vaunting ego, the lost and the winsome, those who might joke or laugh but were inwardly wailing. Onwards they flowed in bright-plumaged tails behind these representative two. And in seeing, I loved them but could not take them. Not one was remotely ready.

That is not to say that they lacked differentiation. Between the two, waves bifurcated. They were Power and Love, you might say, though the one might partake of the other. The one, hearing my silence, became articulate; the other, bathed in her eying, grew sensual. Meanwhile all those of whichever sex in their trail veered this way or that, so that in the end what we saw were two heads of a twinned surge: the blue and pearl-grey, the active and passive, the Promethean and Orphic/Narcissistic. I won't describe savagery: you might sense mass carnage lurking cheek-by-jowl with melodic orgy. Ten thousand beautiful forms lay spread out on the platform, expanding to become the stage for a vast, here-and-now, musically-charged festival, as if to end history. We are ALIVE cried a lyric. The PRESENT is ALL. It is FOREVER, your past and their future *dead*. So we heard. And all the while, to waken a soul from this dream or nightmare came the tramp-tramp of the waiter bringing our bread, a carafe, tomato salad, spaghetti vongole, espressi along with her amaretto biscuits and my favourite pistachio ice cream.

Duce! Duce!' counterpointed 'All You Need Is Love', until at last my reticence was broken by one spare homily, which

Rasputin would transport back to the world as if the Word of a god. Then they decamped. You could see in the mind's eye how on a train back to Paris the one would turn to the other and say, 'He thought you were, like, just some hippy fag, man'; to which the other would respond meditatively, 'I don't know…' behind which lay either yearning or resentment and in both cases a goad towards more power of knowledge. Analogous in the other was recollection of her eyes, which impelled a first sense of being noticed by elegance, Beauty, thus the prick of Eros towards aesthetic fluency. As locomotion beat rhythm over fair fields of France, they would dream as if troubadours in deep consciousness, days of judgement an epoch before them. And when they arrived in a half-forgotten medievalism of the Left Bank, one of my previous pilgrims, now guru in his own right, sat still to listen to them tell of their journey south and to smile in that soft, feline way of his, which from each would evoke the opposite of us, and intone: 'Yes, the last rower and his fairy queen…' To which they would ask, *what*? To which he would set out from his point of view a version of our illustrious pre-history.

Should I rehearse that? Shall I tell you about *me*? I think not, or at least not yet directly. I'm not sure that I can or, if I could, whether it would be accessible, let alone 'true'. In any event, it would be limiting, and I feel limitless. How could I not, given where I began and how I shall end? So I'll recount – and you must take as you will – only in shafts and in fragments.

Decades before, I had known another questor. This was in another city and, alas, the chap is dead. I had almost taken him but in the end let him slip away too. Why? It is not so much that he wore a three-piece and a pince-nez, though they may be indicative. It was, I think, that, unlike the friend who had introduced him, he would turn back too soon from where these ones were headed: experience and *life*, even in books or books of the wilder kind. He had heard music – echoes from those spheres, also off of the street. But he had blocked the wind's howl and cries of strange gods. He had fled the Valkyrie and retreated from heroes, even from potential for the heroic in himself.

He had wanted, he said – or perhaps pretended to believe – to enter the mystery of Time. He had started by searching into lost childhood, but before he had been able to glean much of that age of innocence had come a great war, necessities of adulthood, and intimations of immortality had scattered like shards of a smashed bowl. He had changed cities, migrated north, but in the damp of the greyness all came to seem grim. He loitered in graveyards, absorbing their still, and found he could explain nothing sure to himself but took refuge in an idea that only overall pattern truly mattered.

So he devised patterns, perfected them, sought to live in them. Yet pattern without content has limited value; so groping for content, he rose in his mind, if not being, and, turning again, murmured to himself, 'Let me take you back on my race's journey, back to the olde country, to peasants dancing, Scarborough Fair and so on...' But then, poof! It occurred to him like a scrim falling over a quaint scene that those odd folk, however garlanded in rosemary or scented in thyme, were *dead* now, and you could learn little by seeking to revive them. Even monarchs and gentry, he went on with accuracy, if thin hope; even masters of this past were swept into the grave. (Well-a-day!) Even bending one's knee at Easter could not arrest the process.

He could skry, this questor. He could see shapes beyond surfaces. Hardly superficial, he knew that in fact surfaces are properly ephemeral. The *alt Land* was an origin, but was it a home? What *was* a 'home'? where one had started from? where one alit? where one might end? And when would *that* come? and how? Now? Forever? – He went turning again, again inwardly looking, as if in on himself. Who was he? Mind reverting, he caught on another idea – those wild seascapes of a new world where he had played as a boy: wasn't there wonder in them? Weren't they the true *home*? But the fishermen there had led harsh existences, so hard always, generation after generation, no end to a casting and heaving of nets. And what was the point? Wasn't it all just one unending, mechanical process of bidding farewell and farewell before setting out to sea?

So he pondered, and wondered if he ought to become religious. Yes, he thought: I am seeking a still vantage-point. And casting an eye out for the brief space of time of which such an inward-gazing individual is capable, he sententiously mused: you may try any kind of pseudo-belief, but the Great Work must be to keep searching for the True Path through every alternative. So he stayed fixed to the place he had come to; inert in a convenient, satisfied sense that locale hardly mattered, since nowhere on earth could be quite permanent. And out of the foreign yet familiar elements where he'd planted himself, earth brown and sky grey, precipitation frequent and temperature mild, he occupied Time in envisaging phantoms – intelligences crossing far or near with concerns not dissimilar to his – repeating all the while the mantra that hope may remain so long as one strives to keep seeking in prayer for Right Values. Perhaps inspiration one day could come too, if one were open to It. Meanwhile, being Here, Now and Searching for the True Word and Pattern to conjoin opposites might appease a world webbed of nameless frustrations. Anyhow, it was worth a toss... wasn't it?

8.

SPLENDOUR as object – what is wrong with that? anything? What did I want of them? What was I willing to take? Ach, I feel disinclined to belabour. You judge; I'll confine myself to description. At the least, my beloved could not accept as full quest one that had not partaken of the other. So we came to a far shore of the new world *soi-disant*. And this is what we saw there:

Again young men searching, though this time with young women as lodestar... There was one. She was not of 'good family' but of a kind that our old world might have called Bonapartist. The father, a *capo* in his realm of film, the mother non-submissive, reduced by barbiturates... The child was a wild thing, akin to the boys of my first scene, though moneyed, empowered, ready to inherit the earth. Earth indeed was the element that most defined her: cherry-wood complexion, hair tumbling like mare's mane, eyes enormous and chestnut-coloured, the whites like quail eggs. She wore little ever in canyons she fled to out of megalopolitan Beverly Hills; my darling in some Italian confection could hardly compete. The animal radiance, aura of youth on the wing, free as a eurhythmic dancer; the dark bush of growth under upraised arms, arabesques in motion and belly-dancer's management of a torso she knew how to use to drive young men to tortuous dreams on hot nights under milky ways and fallen stars; to long, pained, unrelievably bounteous voyages up valleys and grottoes of secret creek-beds... In a year or half-decade, at least by age twenty, this girl-woman would know too much, have lived too much to be able to vault a spirit unaffectedly toward diamond skies. But now as she sat by an August Pacific, beneath sentinel flares on a Malibu hill, she possessed just enough ignorant innocence to be able to seem an emissary of some strange god, if not unnameable goddess herself.

We loved the free spirit. How could we not? But one understands destination. However things change, Fate wove her web long ago. Mankind's secret? *Amor fati*, the Romans knew. And in the new Rome of those halcyon years, a free spirit like hers could appear as a fate, or 'body of fate' surely. So this is what happened, barely out of her will, for she had little will then – only *not* to be willed by some parent or other, except one she chose like a dumb, untamed stallion to mount and master the moment. Such challenge! Any I took had to face something like her; nor would Beauty have stayed long were this not so. And on they came, brave contenders. It was like some antique tale in which an Ice-Princess sets up barriers to be melted solely by truest Love. Yet she was no creature of ice, rather of warmth, pastel lava, patent fecundity. They could scent it, the young men, and of course the old. But it was youth that would get her, and lose her, and lose itself thereby, and gain itself too maybe in time.

We were amusing ourselves that year, a decade from my first scene, in the sand on a shore a few miles south of Point Dume.

Aficionados of vistas, we could not help but be impressed by the route up that highway towards that prophetically-named place. As in Venice, there was some illusion of angles which produced an odd magic: look south and you imagined you were facing west; turn west and you were told you were gazing north. The sun off the water came at you unexpected, bringing distant sensations of space holding secrets of time. There are stories – they were rife in that era – of Indian souls who'd gained knowledge cross-legged on nearby cliffs. A Celtic magician, colleague of the pince-nez I've cited, passed in a Pullman car decades before and found himself falling into a trance out of which, for a spell, he imagined he'd gleaned an essential grid for the understanding of human psychology and history. More of that anon. For now we were focused on visions dear to his perception that 'All dreams of the soul end/In a beautiful man's or woman's body'.

Or why not both? In the tomes medievalists call *grimoires*, such words from a sage were illustrated by drawings like the one Da Vinci designated Vitruvian Man. In the sand where we sat under shadows of palm, by a creek-mouth leading into communal woods, replicas in the flesh of Adam Kadmon ambled past. At the lace edge of the waves, silt shimmered under their feet, green glass or blue calm or occasional fierce temper – even madness – of ocean in backdrop. The sky was of an azure glimpsed only rarely west of classical scenes. It silhouetted, especially when sun hung low on the horizon and evening breeze solidified what had deliquesced at midday, these young gods. Here reborn were Hermes, Apollo, Heracles, Dionysus, only to vanish into vapours of infinitude.

One was just like her – just for her, you might say, if observing as we did, connoisseurs reading forms like geometry translated into corporeal shape. How much simpler if humans could be mated à la stud to mare! He was perfect – my darling could see, as could lesser mortals gazing in envy, sentiments in the worst leading to inchoate rage. We speak of love of beauty but rarely of hatred for it, nor embitterment born from it or out of lust or covert moments of longings impossible to conceal. He evoked such a chain of reaction, from the grace of his motions to the glow of his pigment as if in halo. Aquiline eye, *cuirassé esthetique*, proportion of phallus, symmetry of chest, buttock, thigh… Men became pederasts in mind at a glance, then reverted to censorious loathing. Women went soft with a yearning which transformed them to bawds, abject witches; except her. They were Romeo and Juliet, that pair, only coarser – a touch Greek, further adult and alert; a Hollywood stage carried on. We saw Triptolemus in him, the youth elect to go through a cleft in the earth to bring Demeter's daughter back up to a waking world. For a time as twinned bodies met on the shore, in the face of what could be taken as eternity (nor far from facsimiles of Brocken hill), there came an image universal of human sexual ideal. They were *it*: the end and the beginning –

But it smashed. How? Does it matter? Authors in that place a generation before wrote of the 'love-rack' or of dancers who ended by being shot like lamed horses to turn into glue. You ask what happened? to Romeo? Juliet? this Tristan and Isolde? even the Antonys and Cleopatras peeling themselves off sand so that entrepreneurial Octavians could build 'condos' and 'make a killing'? Gone now, all gone, like the sun in midwinter… glorious youth in a cowl, disguised, fugitive, on the lam, taking shelter in dank woods outside dim northern cities… herself sliding down the backside of the Tree of Life, through shells of the Qliphoth, passing like a serpent that bit her – his friend, an Iago, demon lying in wait to undermine Beauty, Success…

She went grey. She took drugs. Her hair became lank and skin pocked. She went on the game. Bitches cruised her, embraced her like a sister, employed her as a mule or a slave, let her risk prison for their errant sakes. She was pregnant – *his* child. The baby may have perished, maybe not. Her father searched for her. Charged with killing her lover, she could not go home again. Would some miracle save her? Should she end up sailing away? Might remorse out of thick clouds form into a spirit, redeemer, some enchanted version of the Apollonian presence she'd imagined she'd glimpsed before Dionysian dispersal had dissolved enthusiasm into a mist?

She turned Christian. I could almost have had her, have taken her – *we*. But… before it could happen, she had vanished like a ghost; like a hope that once was, dead beloved resuscitated, vivid for a flash, for a moment, before receding back in waking consciousness, as in the aftermath of a nightmare, or dream…

7.

VICTORY in pursuit would elude them for years. Other men glimpsed her. She materialized in many minds. Sometimes she was *she*, at other times others. She wore her hair blonde for a season and spoke in clipped accents. She laughed and she smoked, made love like the world might end, then got up and went on her way. In her slipstream, a troupe of existential cripples followed. What do you do with young men who are not of the right sort? I couldn't take them. Why should she?

Following failure, they would grope for excuses. She was evil; she was morally stained. They'd retreat into illusion and give up on life, if life is defined as that quest we've been talking about. Some turned to *machismo*, matey, collective; others went for drink and sank in front of wide screens. Virtual reality – life denial – is a refuge, seductive, from which few re-emerge. Many – most even – opt for that cave. A few compromise in easily-won liaisons with partners who come on like lambs and end up like transgendered rams. Individual self-realization is a rocky pathway; not all can tread it; some who choose to become exhausted old goats. A better departure – more galvanizing – may be to sublimate the process into art, world-beating, even *biznez*: that freak-show of 'wealth creation' by whatever means, which manages not infrequently to yoke social *nous* to covert if not outright contempt for humankind.

A lover rarely takes this direction. I watched one veer from it, being too fair-minded for skulduggery yet too tainted to become a saint. He knew the woman, had his fine moment, deceived himself and lost her like the rest; lost himself too for the bright world and flash employment – a career of 'making money'. He went to ground, as they say. He'd been an 'executive', but don't let that fool you: it's not unknown for the type to have other potentials. In going to seed, he sat in the sun as we did – essential at times to listen to the breeze, to feel its faint sting of chill on your thigh, to bear the subliminal flaying of flesh. You may wander in creek-beds tickled by ferns and caressed by long grasses. You make love to the elements and out of them take a healing to shift you back towards alternative shapes. So he would glean. So he would tell himself, after the fall. And holding him and her in his mind as medallion, he would go in quiet quest into a hermit's cave to 'get in touch with' his soul.

Remember the Buddha and you have a shade of this process – not incantation of *Om* in public but the inward journey of the Brahmin's remarkable son. Setting off with a friend whom he will lose en route; winding through labyrinths of homelessness, penury, the phase of the thief; passing through figurative grottoes, wandering sacred woods until at last he comes up to a face, a vision of other which belongs to him. He glimpses *her*, a girl-woman not unlike my beloved, seated on high divan, painted in garlands of flower and pearl. She is no Ice-Princess but full-lipped and warm-eyed and will recognize and embrace and initiate him into her rites – indeed, so fully that for a time he will grow into being her master: bright shade of me. He will walk in the city and talk with the people. Success will arrive, bringing wealth, celebrity, an aura of power. With them he may grow plump and she pass out of his sphere. The same population will then come to doubt him, disparage, deride what it once reverenced, being fickle but just – the eyes of the world. So they will leave him to face a new illusion: pristine pattern of forefathers dead, though in a version he is obliged again to make his own. So he must doff his fine tunic and go back to the forest to beg. He will sit by a river and weep, then brace himself to feel the breeze. Out of time may come another face like a vision, a form. A boatman, his confrère of youth long since aged, will appear to convey him to the opposite shore, offering shelter, hearing his tale and in the course of it passing on, leaving vocation to him. So he can come at last to ply the waters, study their eddies, assess gusts of wind and transport the weary back and forth, forth and back, until another arrives in whom he will find a reflection, eyes as if caricaturing satyrs or devils long-hidden within. This is his child, come at long last to find him. He is his obverse, to carry on twisting the pattern, rewinding fate along the backside of the Tree into which *she* disappeared long ago, vanished mother, leaving him anguished yet flush with a knowledge of the Whole, as it were: that bitter fruit. Thus he may put up his oar and sit in the sun as we did, eying silhouettes in late afternoon by the shore, hoping for one further glimpse of *their* being: that entity close to perfection...

For a flash, for an hour – that's how it may end, though many have wanted to fix onto permanency. Again the still point, eternal dream, an illusion... The wheel or the phases, cycle or gyre... No doubt there is a centre, if only as defined by what swirls around you. Is it the Zattere in pearl-blue midday? a pattern conceived by a man in pince-nez? a girl on a beach incarnating a goddess? a medallion emblazoning her/him as fused god? a seeker who recollects only to misremember? At what moment do any of these elements become final? Why couldn't I take them? And who am *I*? Does it matter? Who are you that read this? Aren't you and I, at least at some juncture, the same?

Let me tell you: everything passes in and out of a mist. You know that, of course, so is it *I* who have said it or you who have inscribed it here by yourself?

On a far side of that world, still in time with these others, a pessimist tried to gather obscure Truth into a parable about an old man who set out to fish. The old man's life had been poor and his success small, but his eye was still clear and his arm still strong and sense of his craft still finely tuned. His boat was as fit as need be, with lines right for most of what would come. But then arrived the unforeseen. Fate had denied him the great catch and ultimate trophy, until then; so was he prepared for it? At the moment of strike could he hold and stay firm and, in staying firm, hold and, in holding, endure and, in enduring, win? Would Nature defeat him? his own nature, outer nature, a will of some god unknown? Did it matter? Does the conduct of struggle not mean more in the final analysis? Is dignity in defeat not finer than whatever worldly triumph may bring? Who knows the answer? other fishermen on shore? the tourists who watch? he himself? And if he knows for a flash, for an hour, might not epiphany pass in night's chill, hunger, physical pain or the failure ever to make the same fight again? Will the fact that he succeeded once come back as satisfaction, or will the single event drift in memory to seem no more than it has been: a moment long passed and growing pathetic as it recedes into time, becoming cloudy legend, probable myth, a faint shadow of what may have or never have truly been?

The body decays, and the mind. The corpse becomes grass, and then silence and/or the combing and moan of the sea…

6.

BEAUTY I swim towards. But you haven't located me yet. I've been content to elude you, though I suspect something, or more than that, may have entered your psyche by now. In the meantime, I swim. It hardly matters where, or not yet. I am warm here; you need not worry for me.

Think less of one man in a sea of events than of several. At different times, different strokes, different exigencies. Serenity is an object; precision; impulsion through fluid like an arrow through air. But just as the aimed arrow must be aligned for strange winds, so the swimmer must account for unforeseen tides and odd swells. Fate's ways are obscure and Nature inconstant; even a man's inner power may be inscrutable. The questor must reckon and seek to master himself. Confident in this, he may look outwards with more clarity.

So many charlatans have held forth on this topic; all know the allure of consoling heresy. I mentioned a questor determined that purpose should be to keep seeking the Right Path through multiple alternatives. This supposes a right path, which may involve a leap of faith. One of his colleagues, another in pince-nez, decided that multiple uncertainties were an answer – The Answer – and, believing also in pattern, set out to construct a new Tower of Babel representing how *it* might appear in the word of their epoch. A sublime edifice he painstakingly built, ornamented with brilliance and ultimately absurd. Apotheosis of pattern, it reduced content to near nil: accident, puerile obscurity. The Right Path, Answer, even Pattern dissolved into a flow, to a river that ran back between inner and outer without continence, over-spilling its banks, setting its delta to flood, allowing salt water to seep into its fertile marshlands while sources upstream were dammed in self-serving manipulation – the multiple egotisms of a singular Trickster absenting himself above and beyond events to pare his fingernails.

I could not take him, however devoted he was to epic aqueous creation. O, there was form to it, ultimate unity, parts adherent to whole. There was art – too much, maybe – style, anti-content. What was missing? hierarchy? morality? passion? emotion? the ages of man? differentiation in flux? If everything is important, and equally so, then anything is nothing, and vice versa. This is pessimism too, though painted as its obverse: joy in the All. And he *was* joyful, this trickster: a careening, cavorting drunk late at night, singing songs of innocence, happy in love and in LIFE, yet visibly teetering towards the edge of an abyss, peering over and, in the following frame, about to plunge into tears, misery, bleak despair. Every man loves the clown hanging by his fingertips to the ledge of modernism's iconic tower. But the smile in that last frame drifting towards eternity is only a film phantasm, an image out of that miracle realm of great escapes and *Dei ex machinae.*

Turn away from this magical realist, who himself had turned away from a lover of genuine myth, who in time would attempt another representation of 'real world' synthesis. The pair was sequential: there was a premium on radical feints in that day – great-granddad's to you. I've mentioned this other, his senior by years: the old Celt who'd had apprehensions outside of L.A. and then by the sea at Rapallo. *He* let flow phantasy (so he would spell it) to create tableaux like an artist from the *seicento* might have painted on a ceiling for a doge or a pope, or an Elizabethan might have dramatized for a queen, or a novelist of the bourgeois period might have written for his revolutionary 'new man' or a composer of genius might have sought to embody in oratorio, opera, grand *messe* or gigantic symphony. 'Anything less than the all-embracing might be a pretention,' one of his forerunners had said. They knew it, these ones I pause here to cite. He believed it, the one I linger for now.

Him I could have taken. Envisage the grace, consideration, discipline and pain inherent in trying to comprehend the Universal as a whole, and you may begin to see the kind of heroism he had, or megalomania. I've mentioned Da Vinci's Vitruvian Man and concept of where 'all dreams of the soul' end. From a five-pointed star – pentagram, man as Crown of Creation, analogue of true form, unitary, iconic – he would extract an ideal of athlete and sage, of body and spirit swirling together via a vortex into symbols of the Good, the Beautiful and the True. This was about values, not mere vast toleration or cosmic memory, though it partook of them too. In it was anguish: the slash of Christ's wound, Glory scarred, Lucifer fallen (bright angel!), the rise and fall of a luminous spirit, beginning-middle-and-end, a Romanesque arch held high by its keystone, the 'death of a moth'. We are speaking of shape, and harmonic apprehension. We are veering towards ethics, that multiplicity. How can the *one* ever comprehend the *other*? Small men long for a still point and seek it in hermetic retreat; the larger spirit progresses out from his cave to see in the face that confronts him the 'thousand-fold forms', the smile of similitude over infinity in those who are born and must die.

Is this useful, except in a dream? To know the self or the *other*, is it necessary to invoke a new mathematics? to calculate the intersecting planes of time, space, circumstance, sex, look and character? to integrate all their myriad components and zig-zagging attributes? Lazy minds tend to swim quick towards existential shallows. The greater the spirit, the more complex the pattern – that's what he thought, or in a lifetime had learned; because when young he too had longed for simple certitude, or at least the liberating ultimate negation that, if everything is everything, then nothing may be anything, and vice versa.

He inscribed charts. Thought is like composition of music: you need the bars and the staves. It is one thing to improvise, play jazz, elaborate a beat, another to create sounds that adhere satisfactorily and out of fixity move. Man cannot live by determinist forces alone, accident or Fate, powerful and seductive though they may be. Man is bound – doubtless destined – to exercise *will*: a first truth. But how is *will* to be summoned, and why? And if it is formed in one way – say, for black to proceed in a world made for white – how must it present its face? As *mask*. Naked *will* may only succeed when it has multiple outer powers in its favour, which it does rarely. So it is obliged to disguise itself or, if you prefer a less tendentious term, modify. And how does it know what modifying mask to put on? Analyses by *creative mind*. And what in analysis must that *creative mind* seek to play off of or mitigate? The forces beyond self which self does not create but which mold and brand it nevertheless: circumstance; the eyes of the world – *body of fate*.

I've mentioned these, but he skryed them as whirling and interlocking, the four in cyclonic dynamic, ever merging, dividing, reformulating. And the self stands among them, blown as if by four winds, though from each by a breath that is weirdly, obversely also as if emanating out of the self. And here lies an individual starting-point for study of vast expanses of power contributing to impulsion of personalities, careers, and not just those of men but of families, tribes, nations, collectives throughout history… The winds howl. He looks down from his tower, sees the moon, hears the cries of hawk-headed spirits gyring in from the sea. And one night the moon shines, and on another it is dark. And the seasons pass, and the moon cycles turn, so that there in Nature, inconstant, is pattern too. And if inner is as outer, you may begin to conceive of the principles coinciding with great, overarching phases of Time. And, if you could chart both, and their intersections, you might be able to prophesy when and why a Napoleon might be born, or a Christ or a Helen or a Salomé, and why Rome should have fallen or Byzantium rise or Islam come conquering or the Khan of the East, and so on, *und so weiter…*

5.

STRENGTH as a value – I tell you I swim. And this is a marvel: that one simple man should attempt so much. 'Only the greatest obstacle that can be contemplated without despair lures the soul to perfection,' he wrote. Antique maxim. Is it accurate still?

I see another face now. It comes towards me. I am in Café Flore; it is the 1980s. He glides through the door looking important, celebrated, handsome, late and harassed. He wears a beret, a woven wool jacket overlain with a shawl of rough silk, pleated grey flannels and cross-stitched sandals enclosing grey-green-turquoise-yellow striped socks. By these accoutrements you might make out his age. The colours recall hills beyond tarmac he'd set out from in Geneva some hours before.

The airport had been muffled, a touch sleepy under veiled summer light. He was wearing a black t-shirt under his jacket, indicating, I suppose, where he thought he was going or who he wished still to be. Soon he would be elsewhere. Ah, elsewhere – that place you long for until you arrive, and again once it's behind you. Unquiet soul, he could not rest in the present. But then his life had begun in a dark clime, not the classical realms he had dreamt of. His career was in exile: flight from and to. Those who had beaten out deracination, found the great good place and put down new roots, were his ideal. He imagined them content in their vivid preserves, substituting for more pristine existence – there will ever be background and origins, not least for a *rara avis* like him. To transcend, obliterate, become *citoyen du monde* fully – that was the hope. Not a soul remained from his childhood; he could not go home anymore or regain lost time – 'twas in another country and, alas... '*Maman*, when will we meet again? in *dem Land der Sonne Licht nicht schient/ das dunkel nächt'ge Land, daraus Du mich ensandt?*'

It shone where he fretfully longed to be. An earthly landscape just, almost too gorgeous for the world as he knew it, labouring as he did under dun northern skies... He had admired them too once, in capital cities, viewed from his distant starting-point. But those metropoles were careless: they didn't need you, didn't hug you, though they could draw you in for a season or two – in his case a dozen. He had given his best there, had been fêted, and now? He was spent, or would be, or feared he might soon be. Great though he had been – in his sphere *ne plus ultra* – he might vanish and be remembered as little more than a male *traviata* superannuated for the *gioia* he had portrayed. Understanding this, he had cursed his form in the lights and grown bitter, yet carried on. Others were lucky, he imagined, though what is luck of their kind but a façade of good taste wedded to surviv-al instinct? What was the point of northern, civilized ardours except to efface the fog and the chill and call up fictional beau-ties in consolation for loss of the sun?

Could I offer him something? Is it why he'd arrived? He showed the ruthlessness of the fatal in his expression, or the con-trastingly pure. Could I help him find rest, conduct him to a safe haven? Was I the guardian to lead his soul where it wanted to be, fixed in a locale out of which it need not stray any longer, except to the ultimate elsewhere? – No, he was not ready, though his wild Kirghiz eyes betrayed how in time he could be. Half haunt-ed, they searched mine inquiring how one might grow into fate. It was the problem of an era, one he typified, tirelessly vaunting perpetual youth. Why grow old, quenchless vanity whispered, if you are able to mask it?

He poured sugar into tea to sustain energy and ease muscu-lar stress. The caffeine made him edgy, disconsolate, cross. *Old* is the great age, or can be, he wished me to say, thus lead him up from a valley of fear. If those like me had a purpose (but who is like me, you ask), must it not be to deliver some such comforting maxim, ersatz wisdom? To grow old into grace, to transcend into glory – that's the directive he was searching for. What other point could there be in reaching 65, 70, more – even his own critical 45? what value to oneself, to the young (how he loved youth!) to lust like an Aschenbach, to run like a Pentheus, to make a goat-footed fool of oneself? Appear august and proud, potent, invincible, as if the portals would ever open to the prize long-contested; as if such accomplishment might negate inanition... Yet, how?

I said little. The sicky-sweet tea made him burst into extravagant confidence. Art, he declared (the blasé on the *trottoir* swivelled to look), discipline, acquisition of order, training, platitudes of existence – what else could achieve apotheosis? essential wealth? appearance of liberality? access to style? Yes. But in a gutter? *Nyet*. No retrogression into the abjection of origins in his north-eastern waste. But... what if he should fail, one might ask? 'My country did that long ago – yet grandly, obtusely, vengefully when necessary; and that's how I'll go. My place now? *Ecco*: I live near Genova, at sea, off Monte Carlo, by Sardinia, sometimes in Paris, New York. With my accounts in Grand Cayman, Lugano and so on, credit lines out of *Ultima Thule*... But don't let them know it, my public. They must see me as ardent, remote, philanthropic, which is what I am truly. The lives I have pleasured! The souls I have danced for! The bread and circuses I've brought to them! Caviar for the *cognoscenti*... I oppose no man's release. I've burned in my own. They've watched me and learned via my fine artistry: Machiavelli was a nostalgist.'

Well, I took him. So now he is gone, though in his sphere he remains... What was he? a dancer, a singer, reclusive actress? Yes, I took him. He succeeded. So now I swim.

You ask where? But where did he age, or would he have done? – They chat in these places about their dentures. He will never, since I took him. The sea is one's doctor, beloved, redemptor. But more of that, perhaps, in time...

Why am I here, where he wanted to be? But one needn't be *there* to be active; one does here as well. Their chilly conspiracy of a world – it is hardly forever. It is no longer so exclusive as it once was, or empowered...

The man who came towards me believed he'd arrive – needful illusion. Yet he remained of the would-bes, the never-wills, a kind of Gawan out of some Fisher-King tale. I do not deprecate: he *could* see a grail, which proves his quality. If he didn't reach it – well, does it matter? Isn't the ardour of quest the true object? Anyhow, I was too fond of him to exact prolonged agony. The tirelessness, the sureness of vision, no tear occluding an eye – these I admired. And here is a clue, for where do tears come from? poor resistance to wind? bitter weather? *orgasmo* of spirit when overmastered by Beauty, Goodness or Truth? *nostalgie*? *amour de l'impossible*? All such elements, surely, though the best betray little. Art is a closed system, ingesting its tail.

I swim, off that promontory demarcating the harbour. You see it as crowded, but once in the water you're alone with her and the gods – the ones whose domain is beyond that horizon marked by grand ochre rocks. It is enough for me. It would have been for him too, but – he is gone. So I swim for him too... One has known many vistas, much loveliness, but this is sufficient. I am aged. What could I do with twelve foot waves in Kauai or even gently-shaped three foot ones at Malibu? Those are for seekers not yet clear of their goal, still intent on adjusting to Fate's ruthlessness. I adore vistas up that coast; I breathe in their wild western airs and low mountain scents of her canyons. But here – that is to say, back up there, behind town – is much more. Those ruins, that ghost of a prince, foul and marvellous histories individual or collective... Souls of dead Indians spoke to a Celt on a train there; mused to me too on my sojourns nearby. But their whispers couldn't hold us, compelling though they were. He needed the longer narrative, here by a cleft in the earth which leads to the middle of All...

Of course you say, All *is* a moveable entity; and when I'm here by these waters, I'm also *there*, space being time, and on the mountain, which we'll come to, where kindred gold reigns over beatitude. In *that* I can tell you (but you know already, no?) every glory you have ever experienced will merge into a medallion and all points at which you have known the sensation, if only once or one time more in some kind of light, become composite: the final still-point where everything *does* contain Everything and All Nothing. But… in the meantime, I swim.

4.

MERCY calls too. I hear others returning: gods from the far west, northern woods. They will not fade away, those fond spirits of pine, sequoia, manzanilla, madrone. They come down the road from where they set out feelin' bad, though not truly, or never always. Song on their lips, bootheels scattering dust, teenage daughters dancing free-form against a bliss of sheer gold via turquoise, emerald, sienna filigree of summer-warm, enwombing evergreens… And the streams rattling fresh over clattering stones, and the roll and sway of the rivers fed from snowmelt higher up… In canyons of boulders above yellowing hills, the children of sun play; and this one laid down their sound, peering through wired lenses, smiling benignity out of his peppery beard: genial genius of place and spirit of times, a *Zeitgeist*…

I took him, or would take him in course. But here he comes now: watch him saunter on stage without pretence, backgrounded in apparata. He is one of five or of six or seven. No lonesome hero like the Tartar of yore, he is a friend of the people, their voice as if, never his own alone. The others plug in, test amps, make adjustments; a drum-tap, a riff roll and off they careen, simple, regular, in old-fashioned strum, a tune half-recollected from earlier times or further back into lost foreign places. His voice rises unrefined, like everyman's yearning turned inside out, perfected in imperfection. It is male, though not too much so; low yet not indistinguishably high; plangent yet oddly sure of what it is, what intended, what called upon to *mean*. His licks are in kind, instrument and player as one, precise against roughness, actor suited to role, maker merged into making, reward embodied in product, life unified in art.

All presents itself as unaffectedly easy, occurring unbidden, an emanation of grace and no more, effort unneeded to reach its condition, *ex tempore*, consciousness subsumed into a moment of Being. The song rides, the crowd sways, he is Mesmer without menace. Wills amalgamating are stilled, to be transported as one into an aerial sphere. The beat shifting, phenomena float upwards, preparing to soar. Soon all will be in space, starlit, rising towards the pleroma, in sight of bright angels indefinite, heavenly bodies unnamed, luminous nightscapes of planets and galaxies which trail out into greatness: Infinity.

Examine the faces. Here is youth, boy or girl, on the verge of adulthood, not quite arrived. If on solid ground he/she might be progressing through moonlight on foreign sands like satin where waves rise and fall, harmonizing against a susurrus of wind in cork oak, pine scent, percussion of cicada on a full breath of warm air out of the south. In daylight might arrive righteous contempt, narcissistic indignation for the rubble that mars the edge of the paths, even through sacred landscape; but at night as in dreams, in Castalia as if, all is humbled and exalted at the same time. Not to God or the gods or a spirit exact, you can hear inward praying – 'Lord, elevate me.' *Who?* Does it matter? The music disembodied becomes articulate, oracular. Out of dulled existence, beyond quotidian pain – 'elevate me'. Out of thickets of sweat and apprehension, from twists in a trip toward expanding horizons – 'elevate me'. Was it a goddess out there on the rim of the moon? 'Elevate me!' Regardless, progressing, traversing what backstage gurus designate as the nine steps to Unlimited Devotion – social formal, social informal, erotic, intimate, tantric, agape-ic, satori-al, Samadhi-an, death/ego deathly – you hear at last a tune winding back and the crowd, stupefied, realizing what it is hearing again, after unending excursion through the sublime, a thing familiar, this ballad as if recalled from sweet youth or some prior incarnation in a voice mild and real and not so distant from what you or yours or hers or his might have been had she sung, had you played, had his drumsticks or keyboard or apparata been in your capacity, which by this illusion they nearly have been...

Later in weed-scented rooms you will ponder while sitting on plush sofas in plasticized luxury, a smorgasbord alongside and groupies abundant – publicists, go-fers, plate-eyed wannabes – 'How did you accomplish *that*? How did you, like, go out on that adventure, free-float into time way out there in space, and then all of a sudden come back down to earth on the beat at precisely the point where you started out from? Do you count?' And he knows you are riffing and peers into your head with an ingenious grin, Cheshire cat smile like a mask hovering just above many worlds of outflowing forms, each reflecting its other, and replies in a purr words he knows you've already divined, 'Hey man... we gave that up *long* ago...'

So I took him, this one who was also many: rare filmmaker, rough troubadour, anonymous cyclist on a beach. Unlike the previous one, he was no beauty – no Apollo in quest of illusory stopped time, destined to be torn apart à la *Orphée*. The great may be great despite physical deformation, or maybe because of it. Mask and Creative Mind are as essential as Will or Body of Fate. This one too was a *pure*, you could see: fully realized. And that is what was essential for me.

He wore a sign, brand, insignia – skull slashed by lightning, skeleton wreathed in roses. And this is what it said: you have looked into the Eye of Destiny, and Death has seen you. It will take you up gratefully onto a path where vipers crawl into maquis and serpents turn turquoise along the perimeters of rock-pools. Garden colours will glow while far away on a Cadillac green hill lights will bob through scrub pine as they proceed around twisted oaks and down to the lip of the water through fern and bamboo. Tiny night-boats with lanterns rowed by the fishmen are clawed back on a moon path like mermaid's tail, gleaming and glinting towards *her*: the face etched in platinum against a mirage of the Castel Eternal.

The sea sighs. A fountain jets soft and calm on the terrace from which my pool drains into a lily-pad pond. You may cool tired feet here at noon when tall grass has hushed and all life diminished into a *dolce far niente*. In pampas groves further up lies hid a discrete altar. Under date palms, it is silent; and *she* is nearby, alone, next to her pool, our enchantress unheard. Dark is the source out of which her streams flow, phosphorescent, bearing flotsam, a torn warrior's limbs, water cleansing and washing away sanguinary stains, spreading out in a heat-haze under heavy motes of light, amid which no mind stirs…

3.

INTELLIGENCE seeking, in distraction one night I cast north again, and back to the east. On a dead edge of winter, in blue-black and white, stands a city where devastation from war never ceased. Here others were dreaming, labouring, heaving spirits up against adversity, chronic downdrift of elements, soot, unclean air, tainted water, broken heat pipes, rusting girders, rotten root vegetables. Through scrims of cheap lace outer vistas glared bleak, depressive, inculcating dense gloom. Yet paradoxically there seemed to be riches here too, fool's gold or mica in strata of earth beneath ruined graves. Up from the ground glimmered as if in blue flame green-ish, gaseous, flickering reds and ambers along seams of charcoal, ebony, tedious brown-grey. A dirge at a distance, melodic in mood, comes as from deep under earth, bringing chthonic memory in basso profondo, yearning to swell into baritone, even light-world tenor. Enwombed in susurrus of alto, contralto and mezzo in sidereal, it ascends towards on high. Entering the sound, imagination departs crypt or prison, spirals up out of cruelty and in the direction of gates to initiations as yet only hoped for.

Flying west in a brilliant gloaming, it crosses a border into evening lands of those days, alternative cities glowing. One,

Janus-faced, looks back and forth at once, seeming half artificially gorgeous, half grotesquely charred. Here, it might be, is a pivot from which a new whole might be fashioned: a new truth in its falsehood, an old lie in ironical reality. Trolls and gods seem the norm here, easy lives crushed. Yet ease too is on offer: a chance to be narcotized, to drift down into satiny, unsettling torpor. What may escape from such compost? jets of humour? radical thought? defiant passions? courage? What colours against absence might slash *chiaroscuro*? what energies to defeat an Oblomov syndrome?

A hard will to accomplishment stirs in municipal flats. The sight of a beautiful face on a tram, consumptive in furs, evokes visions of tearing diamonds from muck. Music resumes low under old chandeliers, smoke-stained pilasters. Along pallid streets a new expression for old departures is summoned, evocations described, invocation to dead gods, howls of renunciation of all that has been, oppressions of here and now – *Revolution!*

She flies with bared breast and an anarchist flag. She swirls over bodies of dismembered comrades, this Nike triumphant. Out of the stench of methane she appears as futurity, hope, longing for life beyond death, or at least you and me. Yet why is she here? And how does one recognize this terrible beauty, so marble-eyed, cyclically-born? Is it through *him* or another inside you, glimpsed from a past on a page? But then: *he* is here too, in the flesh, as he was in, say, 1990 when the Wall came down and philosophies imploded. He is as he was in some lost century, suited in black with high collar, simulating a preacher of antinomian sect, though with a mildness of eye, geniality of persuasion, kindness of manner, grace without show.

He takes them in, half enchanted, to release them again to perform in a piece that may help you recall some scene half-remembered and / or apprehend a potential to come. Art passing calm over intellectual shards plucks a fragment here, lingers over another there, educes contrast, comparison, stimulates not conclusion so much as fresh thought, intimations – a deeper receptivity. Down in the mind's mulch music plays on: a soundtrack as if to some inner tableau, private vision of what is appearing on his stage. Into your eyes comes an image, through your soul probes a dream, around your heart courses anguish, in your genitals stir aching for what has been or might have been or might still or once more could be.

He puffs a cigarette, watching from a wing. A nerve-wracked soprano stands on the boards. One weeps in mortification over her missed notes while another listens without comprehending. When at last it is over and in smeared grease-paint she bows, dripping mascara onto the orchestra pit, applause is laced with jeering. Through the audience come cat-calls; a man in a tuxedo shrieks 'Schweinerei!'... He drops his cigarette under a toe and, stepping out from the wing, bows deep while inwardly grieving, for the sensibility of his troupe, for his mother long dead, for his son and beloved who cannot sing up to standard but has nonetheless been granted her fifteen minutes of chance. Where is pity? Has he offered her triumph or humiliation? Does he know more than we about how to bend perfection, and when? how to make art fully human? how to summon 'one from the heart'? Has he perhaps gleaned the secret of what lies *beyond*, as have others: this writer, that painter? Has he appreciated the moral of higher attainment and tradition, of innovation in the direction of immortality?

Well, I took him. Flecks of dandruff and ash, distended gut and the rest – I took him. Hypertension et al, this creator for *them*, relentless, happily encumbered with a blind faith – I dragged him laboriously back to my lair.

You may hear cries, lamentations, suppressions at funerals in churches decayed by lack of belief or kept intact by no idea of where else to go. You may glimpse a dark angel leaning over a trench freshly-dug to ask no one within earshot, 'What goes on down there truly?' How could she know, being of the sky? And if That Which Is Above *is* like That Which Is Below, does the revelation amount to much more than one of those old palliatives *grimoires* offered 'magicians' to hold up as cover against their depthless ignorance?

Well, I took him. I hauled him along pathways glimpsed in a dream. I proceeded at sunset, in hopes of recapturing the one I'd once loved. If I did not find her, I thought, not a thing on this earth would be worth any beautiful act. Yet when I came through twisting branches and saw her shade wanly waiting, I felt obliged to kneel like a medieval knight raising his grail to the queen of the skies. Around the four square corners of a circled chapel, tributary altars appeared. But then against rapture came a wild wind, bringing rain and black hail and the dark. Wings beat against my skull, fragile or hard: spirits or bats or ghosts of dead heroes or of the beldam who had posed as the goddess *Amor*. I became not one but many, shattered into in a vast scheme, at different stages, in bifurcating personae, multiplied elements, atomized surface necessities giving way to an ordeal of passing through flame. From beyond came the moans of the drowning at sea, a soft chh chh over pebbles, a drawing back of sad waves, the sighing, the chh chh…

Who was calling to whom there? what phantom as if out of a *paradiso* reformed? what *other* glimpsed in a flash, for an hour, then lost for an hour, then ecstasy for an hour transfiguring all, until consciousness staggers, and the body, though it seems a Divine Mind can carry on ceaseless, *improvistore*, omniform, ever unstill?

2.

WISDOM I've avoided defining. I make no apology for it; ambiguity is of the essence. I've told you I swim. You may one day too, for reasons to infer. I offer no advice; you must do as you will. I will take as I like.

What I take may dissipate in the sea. Inland, it may be laid on a bier or set in a tomb. On the rim of my mountain stands a conical tower; inscriptions mark the walls of its winding stairwell. We all need remembrance; I do have values. You need not share them. Who am I to command?

Imagine, if you like, being at the foot of that stairwell. Naturally it is of stone; of course it is old. Pale and shot through with amber, it is also bright. The passage is narrow; slim windows punctuate each quarter turn. Between them are pictures you may pause to inspect; it is no longer necessary to be swift. The height between steps is irregular, the footing treacherous – take care not to fall. Each picture elaborates a story as if off the page of an illuminated script. The pigments have a glow as of devotional images. Gold shadows their outlines; the stones behind each have been hammered back and are carved with shallow incisions, so there is relief. By every scrawl of a stem or about-face of a flower, you will find words you are tempted to speak. These are or may be as significant or not as the foliage that gently entwines them: it is for you to decide. I won't repeat here what the inscriptions say: you may, if you go there, decipher them. On the other hand, I will indicate what they depict, if only in sketch:

At the first turn is a young king, a boy wearing a crown. At the second a young woman arrives to face him; the two are exchanging talisman rings. At the third, they are enthroned beside one another, presiding over a court. At the fourth a knight mounted rides past their pavilion, milady's scarf encircling the shaft of his lance. At the fifth he is seated ungirdled beside her in a verdant wood; his helmet is off, and she is unclothed. At the sixth he is arraigned before king and full court. At the seventh the queen kneels to plead clemency for him. At the eighth the king, agèd, regards her in penance; his look holds compassion. At the ninth he has turned in solitude to his books. At the tenth he sits at the top of his tower looking out over the endless valley beyond, his hair white and beard grizzled, his visage like that of the Ancient of Days.

His cell at the top is windowed in each of its triangular quadrants. The vale to the west is terraced with vines to its north. On its furthest horizon sun appears to be setting everlastingly. Motes of light fall through glittering dust to the stones at his feet; they are clad in black velvet, the right with a golden sun on its toe, the left with a silver moon. His throne is fashioned out of an oak stump; its back side is rough and has a protrusive knot, a gnarled deformation, on which one may sit. Installed here, he becomes *other*: dark-cowled, aquiline eye spying from under a hood onto eastern gloom, as if searching for prey. As you descend to the ground here, the slit-windows display bleakness or nothing at all, except such demons as the mind may conjure. Between apertures every picture is dim. Tortuous limbs of stunted growth enwrap weird personae: a fantastic sorcerer, fatal woman, an obscene jouster, executioner, a dame so ugly you feel as if you are gazing at the serpent-swathed face of the Medusa. You wind down through spirals of gorgeous lovers now raddled, parents poisoned by jealousy of their offspring, solitaries viewing the world through the eyes of unsuccessful rapists. At last you reach bottom, an underworld of would-bes and never-have-beens agitating in burbling marsh. Among these *misérables* in a land where no sun ever shines, you slog blindly towards a haven, following paths that lead nowhere, choking in rotted woodlands. You are dank to the marrow with the frigid humidity. Here is a realm of the death of the soul.

I am there now. I sit in rags by a stalagmite cathedral, avoided by pilgrims, repulsive in stench. Across a famed river, through an arch of the goddess in triple aspect, I see a house shimmering in halo-ed brilliance. It is a café as if – of *amour*, of *enfants du paradis*, of children of light being taken by poetic mania. From under its gingerbread roofs through gabled windows protrude faces; a play seems to begin, some midsummer night's dream. Eager in declamation, the young men in downy sideburns and with scrappy goatees court young women gorgeous in yellow curls or dark bobs. Incanting stanzas of anguish and hope, concocting theories to pattern desire half-known, these ardent spirits labour up to the edge of a happy exhaustion. Brave dancers in the making, composers, singers, wild fiddlers, directors or impresarios – all of them gleam with the proverbial hard, gem-like flame. I can make them out just, like dying coals on a grate. My eyes are engraved by their naïve imagery. And I take

113

them, celebrate them and in the end trust that they may take me. Because they must now, mustn't they? Because they too will come to this juncture one day and spy what is destined – what promised for a Happy Few.

1.

CROWN to the quest, we are led into the court of the castle. All is arranged so that the altar of the judge is transformed into a podium on a stage. Twin candelabra have been set at either end; an usher, perhaps waiter of yore, steps out to light them. Hush descends. Spirits agitate perceptibly, though nobody moves. A flight of cool air, from where you can't say, and he spreads his arms wide, looking at or through you.

In she comes from a wing where the judge might have waited had court been in session. All lights are dim; sole illumination comes from the candelabra and a spot at the back, trained in a circle onto a space which now seems to open out into a spiral onto what reveals itself as a red-draped proscenium arch.

She might have been anybody you knew. I can no longer say if she was round or was tall, was dark or was fair. I couldn't then either. Her shape – mobile, electric, intense – was as an angel's might be. Or was she demonic? Ambiguity, eternal. It is clear at least that she was possessed of a power, though of what? Can you say? – Certain genius?

The Mona Lisa comes to mind, that obverse portrait, or some iconic female out of, say, Klimt. She was an Ancient of Days, out of Kafka, or the flame in the hand of a statue of Liberty. But I'll give up describing. Here is what she did:

She sang and, as she did, I listened to music as if from inside the vast dome of a mind which might have been mine, or no one's or everybody's. Beyond an owl or a hawk's cry, it consisted of something like the chiming at dusk of small, then large bells in a city unknown and ideal. It echoed up against a sheer face of mountain, steel-bright and snow-peaked, resounding back as strings played – violin, zither, viola, violin-cello, lute, double-bass and so on; then back into liquid runs of electric guitar, pedalled-steel and other, until silence reigned once again. Out of this came a horn call, or was it trumpet fanfare? Either way, it seemed that a brass band then followed, rum-tum and trombone. Drum rolls kept up a beat underneath, then suspended themselves so that you could sense what had failed to arrive. Piccolo flutings wheeled like small birds against sunrise, then came a plangent clarinet, then descent into *hautbois*, then low bassoon exploration of grounds underneath a mulch of damp trodden leaves, colours yellow and brown, pale and hectic red. It was spring again and lime-green returned: chartreuse, emerald and jade. A note in the woodwinds rose, indicating hope; held for three bars, or was it seven or nine? Then, exhausted as an old soubrette on last legs, she broke down via mezzo, contralto, alto coloratura and began slipping away. Or was she reborn, fresh again, impossible to look at without musing on fecundity, reproduction, generations going on and on beyond this ghastly space, echoing re-echoed in voices frail and yet strong in the wings, softened basses, baritone, a sole tenor up on to rafters where mezzo, contralto and alto took it once more and then into the *voix des enfants chantant dans la coupole.*

A shriek or lament through the dome, and all flees. Consciousness shattered, there stood revealed, as if from a core, black-draped as she was, out of violet and ruby and opaline pink, a shape in white light of the blindness to come, envisaged as if out of a glimpse into transfiguration. Was it a child that shimmered there soft? some entity beyond description, not quite definite? infinity circumscribed so that you might comprehend its outline in form? If so, it was gone as soon as she was reconcealed, white light receding into the pink, violet, purple and gentleness enclosing, leaving a muzzy dark space, an indeterminate void, returning you out into the dank reality of shadows, as if in out of a vast outer space.

She vanished. The proscenium arch returned and endless funnel behind it accordioned up until sealed, as if it never has been. The stage reformed into an altar for judge, though none would appear or seem expected. Candelabras extinguished, we watched wisps of smoke ascend towards a smudged, ancient ceiling too high to reveal if any fresco had ever been painted on it. Encrypted again, we make out the walls of our cell and realize that perhaps we are no longer more than aftermath – larvae as if, lost in a damp richness of earth.

La commedia è finita whispers a faint wind, though how could you hear through those hermetic walls? Up there danced the living. You detect sounds of their feet though you can no longer say what they look like – frail or tall, pale or rose-tinted – or what waltzes or polkas or fox-trots or jitterbugs they whirl in, or what precise notes are playing, though you recognize shuffling as in a mind's ear, and echoes of joy of a world you once knew, and in this are assured that in sleep you may rest, and the bright spots can swirl on and on.

How I loved them, you think, and have through this aeon I've come to inhabit: *forever.*

Forget nothing, because the uroborus coils, and 'in your end is your beginning'.

Surely you believe this, *mon semblable* : that the One is fated eternally to return?

London, 2010

www.ingramcontent.com/pod-product-compliance
Lightning Source LLC
Chambersburg PA
CBHW071403170626
46811CB00003B/1242